PRINCESS AVENGER
QUEENMAKERS SAGA I

BY
BERNADETTE ROWLEY

PRINCESS AVENGER
Bernadette Rowley
Copyright © 2019 Bernadette Rowley
All rights reserved.

First published 2012 by Penguin Australia, Destiny Romance Imprint.
Published 2016, 2019 by Bernadette Rowley

ISBN: 978-0-6483105-2-5

Printing/manufacturing information for this book may be found on the last page

First Printing, 2016
Second Printing, 2019
2019 Cover Design by Dar Albert
Interior Design by
Business Communications Management bcm-online.com.au

VC:PA-191012

ACKNOWLEDGEMENTS

To Louise Cusack for her inspiration and advice.

To Sophia James for mentoring me through the early editing of
Princess Avenger.

To MG for being there to bounce ideas off.

To my husband, Michael, and my sons
for their unending love and support and for sharing in
the disappointments and triumphs of a writing life.

DEDICATION

Dedicated to the memory of my father, Jim Garton.

TABLE OF CONTENTS

* * *

CHAPTER 1

PAIN dragged Alecia Zialni of Brightcastle back to awareness. Her face throbbed and hard stones gouged her shoulders. *Cobblestones? And my bow is digging into my spine!* Gentle fingers grazed her left cheek and she froze, willing her body to remain still but unable to slow her racing heart. The sharp metallic odour of blood swamped her senses as her mind sought to explain her situation. The fingers moved from her head to her arms and legs, brisk and practiced, deftly exploring her body for hurts.

She gathered her nerve and opened her eyes. Pain shot through her left temple and she blinked tears away. A man in a charcoal-gray soldier's tunic and black breeches leaned over her, his dark curls falling forward to frame a face all hard planes and straight lines. Gold flecks sparkled in sea-green eyes that reminded her of the stormy ocean at Wildecoast.

"You should be more careful with whom you pick a fight." His deep voice caused a thrill of unease within her. He rose and strode down the cobbled street, his dark cloak swirling against the taut muscles of calves in fitted black leather boots.

Alecia released her trapped breath, mesmerized by the grace with which the soldier moved; more like a stalking wolf than a man. *Where is he going?* And then she saw the body of the burly redhead, the handle of a knife sprouting from his chest, the crude tattoo of a serpent and dagger on his forearm. Alecia's insides clenched at the sound of steel against bone as the dark stranger pulled the blade free, cleaned it on the victim's shirt and slid it into his boot. She glimpsed a ridged scar on the back of her rescuer's left hand as he returned to her side.

Alecia raised tentative fingers to her cheek and pain throbbed through her skull in response. *What has happened?* Jumbled images crowded her mind but she sorted through them and remembered the inn and the mercenary. *I attacked that man in the street and now he is dead!* She peered at the hand the soldier offered her and followed his arm up to eyes that now held more than a trace of impatience. Her heart lurched. The man had likely noted her every feature! She touched her head and sent a quick prayer of thanks to the Goddess. At least her hood still hid her long blonde hair. If only he didn't look too closely at the clothes she wore, perhaps her secret was safe.

"You —" Alecia struggled to speak around the lump in her throat. She swallowed and tried again. "You have my gratitude," she said, her voice husky. She clutched his hand and he pulled her to her feet as if she weighed no more than a child.

The sudden movement sent shooting agony through her skull and she wavered, dizzy, her palms on the silver buttons of his broad chest. The soldier caught her wrists and the hairs on Alecia's arms rose at the contact. Her gaze locked onto the curious amber stone that hung at his throat. It emitted a faint ochre light that flared and then died as she pulled away. Her eyes must be playing tricks.

When the world stopped spinning, she pulled free and straightened the longbow across her shoulders, then stooped to retrieve her quiver and arrows. Her movements caused the soldier to arch one strong dark brow. Alecia's face grew hot. He didn't seem impressed by her armoury.

"You've the look of trouble about you, lad." The soldier, a captain by the insignias on his tunic, stepped closer.

Alecia's heart raced. So far her disguise held, but for how long?

"I'm not looking to cause trouble," she said. "I'll be on my way, if you don't mind." *Damn, why did I ask him for permission?*

"I do mind." The captain's words were low and gruff. "I'd like to know why you picked a fight with a man twice your size."

More like three times, Alecia thought. His closeness made her skin tingle. What was wrong with her? He was just a man; and a soldier at that!

"If you can't explain yourself you must come with me to the prison."

He seized her arm and her body stiffened, heart thudding against her ribs. Any one of her father's soldiers might recognize her.

Alecia pretended to go along with the captain as he walked past the inn toward his horse. As they neared the mouth of Firedrake Alley, the weak midday sun struck the quartz walls of the hilltop castle that gave the town its name. The captain threw up his arm to shield his eyes from the glare and Alecia seized her opportunity. She wrenched her arm from his grasp and bolted between the buildings. The odour of rotten garbage and human waste assailed her nostrils but she barely noticed. This was *her* world.

* * *

Captain Vard Anton swore. Damn, the lad was fast, but he wouldn't get far. Even though Vard wasn't familiar with this part of Brightcastle Town, he did have a nose for a trail, and that nose still twitched with the lad's scent. Was it lavender? He shook his head and started toward the lane. The youth was already halfway to the first crossroads.

"Blast!" The stiff leather of his new military boots pinched his toes. It was typical of Prince Zialni, heir to the throne of Thorius, to supply boots for show rather than comfort. The air was thick with the foul stink of the slop that caked the alley. Each step brought new and hideous smells to his nose but he grasped the amber talisman at his throat, mentally sorted through the jumble of odours and locked onto the faint hint of perfume. Despite the slippery surface, he picked up his pace and was gratified to see that the young man hadn't pulled any further ahead.

If Vard could just stay within sight, the lad would tire soon. He recalled those startling lilac eyes as they stared up at him out of that battered face. Why not just turn around and get back to his horse before some scoundrel rode off on it? But he knew he wouldn't. The sharp prick of instinct told him he needed to discover why the young man had attacked an armed mercenary on a public street in broad daylight.

He slid to a halt in the dirt of the alley and strode forward to the next laneway. His quarry had disappeared. A scrawny dog rifling its way through a pile of refuse sniffed at Vard, whined and ran the other way. Vard smiled. He could still put the canines in their place.

He sent his senses out into the surrounding alleys, searching for a trace of the lad. The faint echoes of a racing human heart drifted back, several alleys toward the town centre. No need to give up yet. That lad needed help and, if Vard's instincts were right, it might well have something to do with the tyrant, Prince Zialni. The groan of a swollen timber window being forced open sounded and he glanced up. The contents of a chamber pot cascaded over his head and down his shoulders, the stench overwhelming. He spat the fetid concoction out of his mouth and wiped his eyes clear in time to see his quarry's amused lilac gaze as the window slammed shut.

* * *

Alecia gasped, hands on knees, her face throbbing in time with her thumping heart. Her left eye had swollen shut. The one person who could help her now was Hetty, her childhood nurse and a gifted healer, who lived on Firedrake Alley. Alecia had circled around and was now only two alleys from where the captain had found her, close to Hetty's.

His gold-flecked eyes burned in her memory. She thought she knew all her father's soldiers, but her dark rescuer was a stranger. Something about him put her on edge, suggested he was neither tame nor civilized. She settled her bow and arrows over her back, feeling for the knives in her belt and right boot. The hard knot of fear in her gut softened at the touch of the weapons.

The hide of her boots made not a sound as she crept to the end of the lane and peered around the corner of a two-storeyed brothel. From here she could see the rear of Hetty's small double-level shack and had a clear view back to the main street. Foot traffic had returned to the market precinct in the short time since she had fled from the captain, but the narrow street that ran behind Hetty's was deserted, except for a whiskered drunk snoring against a wall several doors up.

Alecia crossed the street to Hetty's and climbed onto the edge of the rain barrel, reaching for the handholds below the second-storey window. Once she was high enough to peer over the sill, she removed one hand to give the window a shove. It opened a crack. Alecia grasped the sill, pushed the glass all the way open and pulled herself through. She landed with a soft thump on the wooden floorboards of Hetty's bedchamber and crossed to the window that overlooked Firedrake Alley. Nothing moved down there.

A shoe scuffed against the floorboards and she spun, knife in hand. Hetty stood near the door, wiping her hands on a stained apron, bushy gray eyebrows bristling above eyes so dark they were almost black. Deep wrinkles framed those eyes and wild silver hair spiked unrestrained from her scalp.

"Did your mother never tell you it was bad manners to enter the house of another without permission?" Hetty's low voice rasped from a throat horribly burnt some years ago when Prince Zialni had sentenced her to burning at the stake. The old woman had been one of Alecia's first rescues.

Alecia pulled the cap and hood back to bare her head, flinching as she brushed her injured face. "My mother is dead," she snapped, then instantly regretted her tone. "How did you know it was me?" she said, pointing to her outfit.

Hetty frowned. "You call that a disguise? You were lucky this time, though by the look of that eye, your fortune almost ran out."

Alecia fingered the puffy flesh around her left eye and a wave of nausea struck her. How would she explain the injury to her father? "Please don't lecture me, I feel bad enough already." Her belief in her fighting skills had been misplaced. Twenty-four summers of sheltered royal existence had been no match for the violence of that mercenary.

Hetty dropped her apron and folded her arms beneath her scrawny bosom. "Come down to the kitchen."

She followed Hetty down the stairs and left her bow and quiver in the hall. A small pot bubbled over the fire in the kitchen hearth and the odour of rotten eggs, stinkweed and garlic hung in the room. Hetty shuffled across to the window, drew the heavy curtain and turned up the lamp.

Alecia wandered over to the shelves on the opposite wall. No matter how often she visited Hetty she always had a reluctant fascination for the brains, spiders, eyes and teeth in the glass containers.

Hetty clutched Alecia's arm and pulled her to a seat at the small wooden table in the centre of the room. Her gaze softened as she examined the injuries at close quarters. "I can help you, Princess, but it'll take all my skill." She soaked a snowy cloth with water from a wooden bowl and bathed the crusted blood from the damaged eye.

"Ouch!" Alecia's eyes watered at the sting of bruised flesh and she gripped her knees to stop herself from pushing Hetty away.

"Nearly finished," the old woman said, her gaze gripping Alecia's. "Did he do this to you? The man with the gilded eyes?"

Alecia frowned, recalling the disturbing eyes of the captain. How did her old nurse know of him? "He was my rescuer. One of the mercenaries lies dead."

Hetty reached into her apron pocket, removed a velvet-wrapped object and uncovered a flat amber stone the size of her palm. She dropped it into the pot over the fire, muttering under her breath.

The hairs on Alecia's arms stood up as an orange vapour rose over the pot. She longed to ask what Hetty knew of the captain but the witch would not welcome any interruption.

She suppressed a yelp as Hetty whirled from the fire, virulent ochre mist oozing from the hearth pot that hung from a wooden hook in her hand. The old woman plonked the pan in the centre of the table then removed the stone with wooden tongs, rewrapped it and placed it in her pocket. She poured the concoction onto a saucer, soaked a small piece of linen in the potion, picked it up with the tongs and turned to Alecia.

"That smells terrible." Alecia leaned back in her chair.

"I wouldn't have thought you'd let a small thing like this upset you," Hetty said.

"I am *not* upset," Alecia said, sitting up straight so that Hetty could reach her. "How does it work?"

"Ah, that would be giving away my secrets, and I wouldn't do that unless you were my apprentice. Tilt your head to the side, please." Alecia complied and Hetty laid her poultice over the wounded eye and cheekbone. "It must stay there while the sand timer empties." She dragged the large wooden timer from a hook on the wall and placed it on the table.

Bile rose in Alecia's throat at the smell; she concentrated on the feel of the cloth to distract herself. The gentle warmth of the poultice changed to a tingling. Something was happening but would it be enough to fool her father? "You mentioned the man with the gilded eyes. When did you see him?"

"Hetty doesn't miss much." The old woman shook her wild silver hair. "He chased you into the alley and came here looking for you."

"He came here?" Alecia didn't quite manage to keep the squeak from her voice.

"Yes, he barrelled in as if he owned the place. He charged up the stairs to my bedchamber, asking all sorts of questions about a lad with lilac eyes who fought a mercenary in the square. When he didn't find anyone, he looked as though he would do murder. His eyes turned fully golden, and I don't mind saying he frightened me. I have my little secrets but I'm no match for the likes of him."

"Why would he come here, Hetty?"

The old woman's eyes dropped and she studied her calloused palms.

"Hetty?"

The dark eyes rose again. "I saw him chase you. He would've caught you. I made him think you were in this house."

"What did you do?"

"I emptied my chamber pot over his head and ensorcelled him so he believes he saw you at the window."

"Hetty, he could have throttled you." Alecia's lips twitched at the thought of the dashing captain covered in slop.

"He's one of your father's soldiers. I thought I was safe until he fixed me with those eyes and called me a witch. He knows what I am, Princess."

15

"Does he know what you did?"

"I can't say, but he'll return. He said so. You must be careful. There is something about that one. Something wild."

Alecia chewed her bottom lip, the cloth on her face forgotten. She recalled the unease she'd felt when he spoke to her. A sixth sense warned her he was more dangerous than the mercenary he had killed. Alecia had never seen Hetty frightened, even when she had been tried for sorcery. The witch maintained her anonymity with a thin veneer of magic that changed her appearance, but if the captain knew her true identity, she was in danger. What to do? Housing was scarce in the town and Hetty was fiercely independent. She would not want to leave her home.

"Let's see what we have under this cloth." The old woman slid the linen from Alecia's face, her eyes darting over the area around the damaged cheek. Then she lifted a silver-edged mirror from the table. What Alecia saw astounded her. All the puffiness and most of the bruising had vanished, leaving the soft skin of her cheek and temple near perfect. Her left eye looked back at her with a clear lilac gaze.

"Thank you, Hetty. A little powder and rouge and Father won't suspect a thing. I owe you a huge debt for the potion and for risking yourself with the captain."

Hetty shook her head. "It's nothing you wouldn't do for me, child, or that you haven't already done."

Alecia smiled. "Where will you go?"

"I'm going nowhere, Princess."

Alecia shook her head. "He will come back. He said so."

"I'll not run from him or anyone else," Hetty said, a familiar stubborn set to her jaw.

"No, you must listen to me. You're not safe here —"

"Don't fret," Hetty said. "I've enough tricks up my sleeve to fool a stupid man."

Alecia couldn't believe her ears. "You said you were scared. So am I. I don't want anything to happen to you."

"Then stay away. Now you must go." She pulled Alecia up from the table, her grip strong for one so withered. Alecia barely had time to collect her bow and quiver as she was ushered to the back door. The witch unlocked the heavy metal padlock, slid the bolt aside and peered into the alley.

Alecia slung her weapons about her person and checked her knives, reluctant to leave.

"It's clear," Hetty said, and while Alecia still struggled to think of a way to keep Hetty safe, the old woman shoved her through the door and slammed it in her face.

* * *

The barracks of the Prince's Guard lay just inside the castle walls. Vard dismounted and tossed his reins to a groom. Swift, his brown horse, shied away as Vard handed him over, bringing the familiar surge of frustration and sadness. After ten years of training, the gelding still feared him and Vard had to face the fact that despite all his careful nurturing, the horse would never overcome its instinctive terror. It was just another price he had to pay as a member of the ancient and mysterious order to which he belonged.

Defenders were destined to live out their lives in isolation and secrecy while protecting the innocent. It was a high price to pay, and as Vard was yet to find a mentor, he risked losing his human core with every transformation – and, worse, he endangered those around him.

The stench of human waste soured Vard's stomach as he swept the soiled cloak from his shoulders and hurled it into the bonfire. His shirt and tunic followed. Clad only in fitted black breeches and boots, he grabbed a pail of water that lay near the flames and tossed it over his head. Goosebumps sprouted on his chest and shoulders.

A crowd of soldiers laughed. Vard ground his teeth; he must reek if his misfortune had come to the notice of men who only washed when it rained.

"Bring me a cake of soap," he said to a gawky youth who didn't seem old enough to be free of his mother's apron strings. He'd probably lied about his age to join the army. The boy scampered to obey and then stood watching.

Vard soaped his hair and upper body and rinsed with a second bucket. The stink was a little less, but he'd smell like the inside of a chamber pot for the next week. He bent to collect his weapons and found the boy still stared.

"What are you doing here, boy?" Vard asked. "You can't have seen your fifteenth summer."

"I'm thirteen, sir. Prince Zialni took me instead of the shield money my mam owed him. Said he'd come and take one of her boys every year that she couldn't pay. He'll do it too, sir." The boy's voice trailed off as he realized he could be flogged for his words.

Vard felt the tug he always did when an innocent was at risk. "Am I right in thinking your tenure here is unpaid?" He gripped the talisman at his throat, seeking the inner calm of the wolf to control his anger.

"The prince feeds and clothes me and gives me a place to sleep, but there are no wages to send back to Mam. Things are terrible hard for her, Captain."

Vard reached into the pocket of his breeches and pulled out a silver penny, which he shoved into the boy's grimy hand. "You give this to your mam," he said gruffly.

Tears welled in the lad's eyes as he clutched the coin to his chest. "Thank you, Captain." He looked around fearfully. "I better go. The sergeant beats me if he catches me slacking." He dipped his head to Vard and jogged away to the smithy that lay beside the barracks.

"What's your name, boy?"

"Billy," the lad replied, before ducking through the wide door into the shadows of the forge.

Vard turned to stare at the miraculous shining walls of the castle above him; walls that had given Brightcastle its name and were rumored to have been magic-wrought centuries ago. Today they seemed just like their master, their flashy exterior hiding a cold, cruel heart. Billy's wasn't the first tale of its type he'd heard since his arrival in Brightcastle. Rumors abounded of beatings and hangings of common folk for little reason. The familiar rage burned in Vard's gut, inspired by Zialni's cruelty. The man deserved death and Vard would be only too happy to oblige, once he'd figured out the when and the how. He gritted his teeth and closed his eyes. He had to remain calm.

The rage subsided and Vard strode to his room in the barracks, shedding his breeches and donning a fresh pair. The odour of the chamber pot swirled up his nostrils and he thought of the lad he'd chased that morning. His quarry had taken refuge in the house of a witch. Vard had heard whispers of bold rescues of prisoners, including one of a witch whom the prince had ordered burnt at the stake. Was the lad somehow linked with the rescues, or just a stupid young man who had interfered with someone too powerful? He shook his head, the familiar tightening of his gut warning him that he wouldn't be able to walk away from this mystery. He had to find that young man, and the witch was the key.

CHAPTER 2

CONCERN for Hetty gnawed at Alecia as she made her way back to the modest castle that lay on a low rise on the outskirts of Brightcastle town. Hetty had shut her out but she would find a way to keep watch over her old friend.

She located the trapdoor, carefully concealed amongst a stand of trees that grew twenty paces outside the west wall of the castle. Alecia lifted the hatch and descended the rough stone stairs, drawing the door after her. The passage plunged into darkness and she groped for a torch from the pile against the wall, lighting it with her flint. Her shadow cavorted on the damp stone as she traveled from west to east within the wall of the castle, up a narrow stairway and along a cramped corridor to a hinged panel. Alecia placed her ear to the stone but heard not a sound. She stripped off her disguise and felt along the stone for the trigger. A section of the wall swung into the passageway. She slipped through the narrow opening and pushed past the tapestry of the warrior queen. The panel of stone slid back in place with a low grinding.

A fire crackled in the hearth of her bedchamber. She rang for a bath and, while the servants carted the hot water in, she fetched her favorite lilac gown and a change of underwear. Finally, all was prepared and she slipped into the bath, savouring the warmth that eased away the worries and soreness brought on by her adventures.

But, once her attendants left her alone, wave after wave of shudders racked her body despite the warm water. Memories of the burley mercenary returned, his fist slamming into her cheek again and again, causing damage much deeper than any Hetty had healed. Nothing in her weapons training had prepared her for the shock of his attack on her person. He could not harm her now, the captain had seen to that. Could she pull together the shreds of her confidence and go on?

Already she doubted she could continue her plan of revenge against the murderous swine who had killed Jorge. Sweet, brave, honorable Jorge, had merely been defending his parents and been killed last month by a pack of mercenaries sent by her father. The dead mercenary was one of the group responsible for the crime. Tears sprang to her eyes at the thought of her lost love and the chaste kisses they had shared. Theirs had been a love beyond reproach and he had been stolen from her. She had vowed to retaliate, but she had not expected to feel … guilt and … pain at the death of a killer. Alecia's gut clenched at the thought that four of the men responsible still lived. *I must go on, but I do not know if I can.* The thought of those men walking while Jorge was cold and dead in the ground made fury burn away her fear. *I have eight years of arms training! I must just be harder; as hard as the captain.*

Unbidden, his gold-flecked eyes popped into her mind and she shivered. The spark his touch had evoked made her uneasy. Was it just that strangers did not usually touch a princess? The captain was an altogether different species; a man who would do as he pleased and, she suspected, who was accustomed to having his own way.

What if he deduced her identity? If he were canny enough to divine Hetty's true self it would take great care on Alecia's part to stay out of his clutches. She had one advantage: she knew him now, and that would make it easier to avoid him. His eyes again came to mind and her spark of optimism died. She suspected he wouldn't rest until he solved the puzzle of the youth who had attacked the mercenary and dumped the chamber pot on his head.

Alecia studied her reflection in the huge gilded mirror outside the dining room. Strings of pearls were intertwined around loops of her long blonde hair and piled high in the latest Kingdom style. A marquise diamond, suspended from a gold chain, rested like a glistening tear upon her forehead. The lavender silk of the gown left her milky shoulders bare while the fitted bodice emphasized her full bosom, displaying an almost indecent amount of cleavage. Silver beading on the bodice and skirt caught the light, and full lace sleeves almost hid her hands. She wore no jewellery other than the diamond on her brow.

She examined her left eye. A few deft touches with powder and kohl liner concealed the faint traces of her fight this morning. Her father would never notice. She smiled at the junior page who waited to admit her and he pulled open the door. Alecia stepped over the threshold.

Shadows danced in the flickering light of the three candles on the long dining table. As usual, Alecia's eye was drawn to the tapestries and paintings depicting Zialni ancestors in various scenes of battle and ceremony. A portrait of the King, her father's older brother, hung above the fireplace. Alecia's father, Prince Jiseve Zialni, sat at the far end of the table below the portrait. There was a close resemblance in the sharp blue eyes and strong jaw, however King Beniel's hair and beard were golden, while the prince's was almost black. She frowned as she stared at the painting of her uncle, with his open countenance and ready smile. It was in stark contrast to her father, who had become withdrawn and secretive in the four years following her mother's death.

The prince's head tilted toward his advisor, Lord Giornan Finus, who sat at his right hand. Alecia allowed her eyes to rest on the elderly lord for a moment. Since Finus's arrival in the realm, her father had become brutally obsessed with the trappings of wealth, to the detriment of his people. If not for Finus, Prince Zialni would still be a benevolent monarch. Instead, the prince collected exorbitant taxes from the populace in a constant quest to maintain his lifestyle. Alecia abhorred Finus and his influence, spending much of her free time trying to restore the balance of justice as she saw it. She was losing the battle.

Feeling eyes upon her, Alecia glanced at the seat to her father's left and the breath caught in her throat. The piercing gaze of her dark rescuer trapped her. Why was he here, in her home, at her table, on the very day she had slipped his grasp and vowed to avoid him? This could be no coincidence. *My secret is out!* The room lurched and Alecia staggered toward the nearest chair. The captain was on his feet and at her side as if by magic, his palm cupping her elbow and his other hand at her waist.

Twice in the one day he had laid hands upon her, and now his heat seared through the flimsy fabric of her gown. He was so hot! Alecia did not look at his face, desperate to delay the moment when her deception, her crime, would be exposed. She took a deep breath and squared her shoulders. The prince's expression had moved from one of pride in his daughter to distaste.

"I'm sorry, Father," Alecia said, her voice breathy without her even trying to make it so. "I haven't eaten since breakfast and felt light-headed." She turned to the captain and stared into the buttons on his chest. "Thank you. I am now recovered."

"Vard Anton at your service, Your Highness," he said, his voice rumbling through her core. "Allow me." He pulled the nearest chair from the table and seated her before bowing and returning to his seat.

"I hope you are well, Princess Alecia," Lord Finus said. The advisor's smile didn't quite reach his cold dark eyes. *He* hadn't moved a muscle when she had stumbled.

Alecia nodded at the despicable man and returned her attention to her father. *No need to panic.*

Prince Zialni stared at Alecia and for a moment she thought her carefully wrought schemes would come crashing down, but then he smiled. "Our guest tonight, Alecia, is Captain Vard Anton, recently come into my service as leader of my guard. Your cousin Piotr recommended him."

Yes, but why is he here? Alecia thought.

"It's an honor to make your acquaintance, Princess." Captain Anton's black hair brushed the collar of his dark gray uniform and his eyes glowed faintly. The room was quite dim. If she stayed far enough away, he might not recognize her. Her heart fell at the stupidity of her thoughts. *He knows, he has to.*

Alecia nodded, keeping her eyes downcast. "Thank you again for your help, Captain."

"Let us enjoy our meal and afterwards, Anton, you and I will talk," Prince Zialni said.

Alecia let out her breath then began to worry about the subject of her father's conversation. *Please, Goddess, let it just be business.* She shook her head and glanced up to find the captain's eyes upon her.

The meal arrived at that moment: warm crusty bread with spicy vegetable soup, roast pheasant and boiled potatoes. Alecia had started on her soup before her father cleared his throat.

"Captain Anton will think us uncouth if we do not give thanks, Daughter," he said, his brows drawn in disapproval. "If you would be so kind, Alecia."

Her face grew hot. How could she be such a ninny as to draw further attention to herself? She crossed her arms over her chest, hands on shoulders, and bowed her head. "May the Mother, who shelters all, continue to bestow her benevolence upon us, Praise her Holy Name."

The men echoed her words. "Praise her Holy Name."

Alecia shot a glance at her father and saw speculation in his eyes. He would wonder at her odd behaviour. She lowered her head to the meal and didn't raise it until the servant came to clear the dishes. Dried and sweetened fruit with thick custard completed the meal.

"Take care, Daughter," the prince said. "A healthy appetite is frowned upon in a good wife; it spoils the figure. One day soon we shall have to find a husband for you and I would not wish you to make the task more difficult."

This time the heat in Alecia's skin was generated from anger as much as embarrassment. *How dare he mock me?*

The captain sat, his posture stiff, an unreadable expression on his face. "I don't believe it will be difficult to find a husband for a daughter with such obvious charms," he said, his eyes lifting to hers.

Alecia flashed him a smile at the compliment but gratitude was soon replaced by irritation. They discussed her as though she were a prize cow. She cleared her throat, intent on forestalling the subject of her betrothal. Her father spoke first.

"Perhaps you can help me in that task, Captain," the prince said.

Alecia choked on her wine, appalled at the turn of the conversation. She looked at the captain. If he was stiff before, he now appeared ready to fight. Was it attack or defence he anticipated?

"I don't understand, Your Highness," Vard Anton said.

"Be at ease," Prince Zialni said. "I refer to the reason I have asked you here tonight. I have cause to fear for the safety of my daughter, and the incident in the market square this morning only heightens my anxiety. It is indeed fortunate that you were present to aid the luckless citizen after he was attacked. I cannot believe Brightcastle houses such ruffians that would assault an unarmed lad."

Alecia gasped. Relief that her secret appeared safe was swamped by the fear that Captain Anton might readily link the lad and the princess if the incident were discussed in her presence. If that happened, would he expose her now or confront her later? He had not reported the true facts of the incident. *Why?*

"Alecia, dear, I know this news must come as a shock, but there is no need to fear." Prince Zialni turned to the captain. "The princess is my only child. She must live to marry and produce a son who might one day be King. I wish for you to accept the charge of keeping her safe, whatever that entails."

Alecia muffled a second gasp, her eyes wide as she waited for the captain's response. Vard Anton sat stock still, his knuckles white on the spoon that was raised halfway to his mouth. A small muscle at his jaw tightened as he lifted his eyes to the prince. Alecia could not spare more than a thought for his discomfiture when she faced the prospect of the coming days in his company. *How am I to avoid him now?*

Prince Zialni frowned, spinning the goblet in his hand. "I am waiting."

Still the captain remained silent and Prince Zialni slowly stood. Alecia held her breath, sure that one of her father's famous rages threatened. Why did the he not speak?

At last, Vard Anton seemed to come out of his trance and looked at the prince. "I'm sorry, Your Highness. I'll be honored to see to the safety of the princess, should you wish it."

Prince Zialni's frown deepened as he seated himself. "We shall adjourn to the smoking room. There is no need for Alecia to be concerned with the arrangements. It will suffice for her to know she is protected."

Alecia rose from the table. The captain stood while Lord Finus and the prince remained seated. "Please excuse me, gentlemen," Alecia said. "I will retire."

"Until we meet again, Princess," Captain Anton said, bowing. "Sweet dreams."

There were murmurs from the prince and his advisor but she had no ears for them. All Alecia could concentrate on was leaving the room without falling over her skirts. She swept past the page without her customary goodnight and fled up the central staircase to her room.

* * *

Vard stalked back to his quarters in the guard barracks, hand grasping the smooth stone at his neck, his mind in turmoil. He liked having the element of surprise on his side, not used against him, and he could well do without minding a spoiled prince's daughter, no matter how appealing. And she *had* been tempting in the lavender silk and lace that emphasized her tiny waist and revealed an expanse of generous bosom. She was perhaps a little thinner than he generally liked, but that stunning smile transformed her; made him forget her imperfections.

She had seemed discomforted at his presence, which puzzled him. Perhaps she was embarrassed that he had seen her stumble. She had barely raised her eyes all night. He usually had the opposite effect on women. They were drawn to him like moths to a flame; and his flame was just as likely to burn. That was why he kept his distance. Involvement with Vard Anton could only lead to harm. Therein lay the danger of this latest task, but if he could protect the princess while remaining aloof, she'd be safe from him and from whomever sought to harm her.

Vard frowned. He was fooling himself. It wouldn't be easy, perhaps not even possible to walk the fine line between protecting the princess and placing her at risk; already her smile danced in his memory. He recalled the sway of Alecia's hips when she left the dining hall. There was something familiar about her that eluded him. The nagging feeling that he had met her before wouldn't go away, but that was absurd. He'd only been in Brightcastle for a week and had certainly had no opportunity to see the princess, let alone meet her.

He grunted at the track his thoughts had taken. His job was to protect Alecia Zialni. While he kept her safe, he could gather information for the mission that had really brought him to Brightcastle: the assassination of the prince. The truth of his task made him pause. Yes, it met his Defender goals – to protect the innocent from harm by whatever means necessary – but who was the faceless man who had hired him? Was it perhaps Zialni's nephew Piotr? It made sense that Piotr, next in line to the throne, might want Zialni dead, but would the death of the prince bring even greater danger to Princess Alecia? How could Vard accomplish his task and extract himself while ensuring the princess was safe?

Vard rubbed the short hairs across the back of his neck. The zigzag of his thoughts unnerved him. Disaster would surely find him if he couldn't keep his thoughts where they needed to be. Rigid discipline had served him well in the past; allowing emotions to dominate his actions could only lead to ruin. He'd fought too hard to lose himself now.

He pulled his saddlebags from under the cot and packed his clothes for the move into the castle. Vard called his lieutenant in to inform him he'd be taking over leadership of the Zialni Royal Guard, then stepped into the night. As he re-entered the palace grounds, he glanced up to the windows on the second floor of the west wing where the royal family had their suites. Only one room showed a dim light.

Vard entered via the servants' access, left his saddlebags and boots in the utility hall and slipped through the darkened passageways to the main staircase. Phasing partially to exploit the heightened senses of the wolf, his nose led him to the prince's quarters at the end of the west wing on the second floor. The heavy wooden door swung on silent hinges and he pulled it closed behind him, pausing to get his bearings in the near dark. No noise came from the parlor or the bedchamber beyond. Vard memorized the position of each piece of furniture, searching for weapons in both rooms. A short bow hung from a hook beside the armchair in the parlor and he discovered a sword resting against the wall behind the bed.

Footsteps echoed from the hall followed by the squeak of a hinge. He ghosted to the bedroom window, opened it and slid through. Fingers gripping the windowsill, he scrambled for toe holds on the slippery quartz walls of the palace. Finally, his feet found two precarious cracks. He gripped the amber talisman with his right hand and began to form the image of the hawk in his mind.

* * *

Alecia pulled her head back into her bedroom from the hall. "Sweet dreams!" She kicked her skirts as she stalked to the fireplace. "As if anyone can sleep with him downstairs."

Millie, her chambermaid, had been bubbling with excitement at the news that the enigmatic Vard Anton had moved into one of the servant's rooms on the ground floor of the east wing. Alecia shook her head. *Why does he have to be here in the castle? Aren't the royal guard barracks close enough?* Obviously not in the mind of her father. She gazed into the fire, her thoughts troubled and hands pressed to her stomach to quiet the fluttering. What was this reaction every time she thought of him? Fear? Unbidden, his face danced in her mind, uncompromising and confident. He had saved her life and hidden the true facts about the attack. Why had he not revealed that it had been the mercenary who had been the victim, not the lad? It did not make sense.

She poured herself a goblet of deep red burgundy and took a gulp. The heavy wine burned all the way to her stomach. Raw her nerves might be after the surprises at dinner, but at least her part in the mercenary death remained hidden. Had she concealed her shock from the captain? Would he wonder at her behaviour? She needed to keep her distance and that would hardly be possible now that she was under his nose night and day. How could she prevent him discovering her other life, let alone her plan to avenge Jorge?

The thought of Jorge made her heart ache. Why hadn't she been able to save him like she had Hetty? Why hadn't she told Jorge how much he meant to her? She placed the wine back beside the decanter and turned to the fire, staring into the flames. It was too late. Jorge was gone and there was nothing she could do to bring him back.

The remaining four murderers must not escape justice, but who would deliver it to them? Her encounter with the mercenary this morning had shown how unprepared she was for a confrontation with seasoned fighters. Perhaps she would never be ready. If not for Captain Anton…

There was a knock at her door. Alecia's heart sped as the sharp sound intruded. Until today, she hadn't been afraid of anything. She crossed her small sitting room and opened the door. Squire Ramón Zorba stood on the threshold. He had replaced Jorge as squire after Jorge's murder and it was Ramón's heartfelt desire to replace Jorge in her affections as well.

"Where were you at dinner?" she asked, noticing how the midnight-blue velvet of his tunic and breeches set off his eyes and contrasted with the golden waves of his hair.

Ramón glowered. "Your father told me not to attend dinner. Was that on your request?"

"Of course not." She paused, chewing her lip. "Captain Anton was there. Do you know anything of him?"

Ramón frowned. "He rescued a citizen in the square this morning."

"Yes." She shivered. "Have you met him?"

"No, but he has made an impression in his short time at Brightcastle. Only a week and it seems he is already a legend."

Alecia had never before heard the bitter note in his voice. "Why do you dislike him?"

"There is something about the man that makes my skin crawl." Ramón's voice hadn't lost its harsh edge.

Alecia recalled her feelings at her first encounter with the him and her discomforting memories since. "Father has made him my protector."

Ramón's eyes bulged and he tugged on the long hair at his forehead. "Then you must beware."

"Thank you for setting my mind at rest," she said, her voice thick with sarcasm.

"Just take care," Ramón said. "I'll try to keep watch on him… and you." He stepped back into the shadows of the hall. "Perhaps we can practice the sword in the morning?"

She flinched at the thought of sharp steel slicing through flesh. "I think I would prefer the archery range."

"I'll have the horses saddled and waiting at the usual time." Ramón bowed and headed for the staircase and his room in the east tower.

"A curious pastime for a princess," a deep voice said from the shadows at the other end of the hallway.

Alecia's hand flew to her throat and she spun to face the voice, knowing whom she would see. Captain Anton pushed himself away from the wall and walked toward her, his eyes reflecting the light that spilled from her rooms. The grace of his movement mesmerized her. It seemed he slid from shadow to shadow, as one with the dark. She swallowed the lump in her throat. "You startled me."

The captain advanced to within a pace and swept a bow. The faint smell of musk and cloves wafted to her. She breathed deeply.

"Is it customary for you to meet men in darkened hallways, Princess?"

Alecia met his gaze squarely, glad that the light behind cloaked her face in darkness. Her unusual eye color would be impossible to read and that was the feature most likely to give her secret away. "Squire Ramón and I are friends," she said. "Nothing more."

"What is this I hear about archery practice tomorrow?"

"Merely an exercise to keep me from boredom."

"And your father knows of this?"

Alecia cleared her throat. "I do not know."

"There should be no need to trouble him as long as *I* accompany you." His eyes glowed, the gold flecks prominent.

Alecia's chin rose and she stared at him, desperate to find some way she could refuse. There was none. "As you wish, Captain."

He reached for her right hand and raised it to his lips. The kiss was light but he held her hand for a few moments longer than necessary while he stared into her eyes. Her heart fluttered in her chest and she held her breath, waiting for him to release her hand and break the spell.

"Until tomorrow, Princess." He returned to the shadows.

Alecia stepped back into her room. The door closed with a sharp click. Heart pounding, she forced herself to take deep breaths, but they did little to restore her composure. The feel of his lips lingered on her skin. What was wrong with her? She stalked over to the pitcher, poured cold water and scrubbed her hand until the skin was red.

Instinct told her the truth of Ramón's words. Captain Anton was dangerous, and in ways that the squire did not yet suspect. She could not avoid him altogether. Her father had seen to that. All she could do to protect her identity was to spend as little time in his company as possible.

CHAPTER 3

ALECIA awoke to the soft squeak of a door hinge. Heart pounding, she sat up, the bedclothes clutched to her chest. The vestiges of a nightmare fogged her thoughts and a twinge behind her eyes warned of an impending headache.

"Who is there?" she asked.

Millie, her chambermaid, came into view, a lantern held before her. Alecia's stomach growled as the smell of hot, sweet rolls wafted to her from the tray the maid carried.

"It's only me, Your Highness," Millie said. "Who else would dare enter your chambers uninvited?"

Alecia frowned. She had to be more careful of her words or she would have the servants gossiping. "Sorry, Millie," she said. "I had a horrible dream and have awoken badly." The nightmare felt like one of her true dreams; surely the enormous brown bear belonged only in her imagination. She shuddered at the thought of facing that nightmare in the cold light of day.

"Let me get the candles lit, Highness." Millie continued across the room and laid the tray on the small breakfast table by the window then bustled about lighting candles from a taper.

Alecia massaged her temples as she watched the flames flicker in the light breeze caused by Millie's movements. The maid pulled the heavy drapes aside to reveal the soft glimmer of dawn. A rooster crowed and a faint answer echoed from the town.

"I think a fine day is ahead," said Millie, turning as Alecia climbed out of bed. "You do look awful, Princess, if you don't mind my saying."

Alecia did mind. She retrieved a hot roll from the tray and bit into it. Surely food in her stomach would banish the ache in her head? "That will be all, Millie. I'll dress myself this morning." She handed the maid a sheet of parchment folded and closed with her personal seal. "Please give this to Squire Ramón as soon as you leave me."

Millie tucked the paper in her apron. "Captain Anton is already up and about. Have you seen him, Highness? There's something about him that makes it hard to breathe."

"Yes, Millie," Alecia said. "I suggest you be about your chores."

Millie blushed. "Yes, Princess." The maid scurried toward the door and stepped into the hall, the lantern held before her. Alecia followed, wondering if the captain still patrolled the hall as he had last night. A shadow moved near the end of the passageway. The shiver up her spine told her it was her dark protector who prowled the hall.

She slipped back into her room, closed the door and crossed to the huge carved wardrobe. The soft gray breeches and matching shirt should do for an early ride to the archery range. Her father disapproved of breeches but Alecia revelled in the freedom of movement they allowed.

Once dressed, she checked her appearance in the large mirror on the front of the wardrobe. The snug fit of the breeches showed off her long legs and tiny waist. She smiled, wondering what Captain Anton would make of the outfit, and then shook her head; Jorge was not dead two months and here she was wondering about another man. It was wrong, wrong, wrong! Taking her wayward thoughts in hand, she pulled a deep gray wool-lined cape from a hook on the side of the wardrobe and slung it about her shoulders. It would be chilly on the ride and the dark cloak would make the lilac of her eyes look closer to blue. Her long blonde hair she left to cascade around her face.

Alecia slung the shortened longbow across her body and the quiver over her shoulder. The tapestry that covered the door to the hidden passage caught her attention. It featured a young woman, sword in hand, her flaxen locks restrained by a golden crown. Her mother had told her the queen was a Zialni monarch, called Izebel, from a time long ago when women ruled the land. It had been Izebel's daughter Daphini who had brought the kingdom to its knees, precipitating an uprising that had seen Daphini's brother take the throne. Kings had ruled the Kingdom of Thorius ever since. Alecia dreamed of becoming a warrior queen who led her soldiers into battle and wiped evil from the face of the kingdom. She had vowed that one day, queens would again rule.

A knock at the door jerked Alecia out of her reverie. Fearing it was Vard Anton come to fetch her, she flicked the tapestry aside and triggered the hidden catch. She entered the passageway and flattened herself against the inside wall, praying to the Mother that the panel would close in time. Seconds seemed like minutes as the low grinding of stone on stone filled her ears. Finally, the wall settled back into place. The captain would not dare enter her chambers. Would he? If any sound penetrated to the passage, her rasping breath and pounding heart drowned it out. After a tense moment, she allowed her body to relax.

"That was close." She pushed off the panel and headed along the narrow corridor that would take her to the trapdoor hidden outside the castle walls. Ramón would be waiting in the park nearby as per her note. She made the trip in darkness, feeling her way as she had done many times in the past, barely noticing the creatures that scuttled out of her way.

Alecia shoved against the trapdoor and climbed into the faint light of dawn, half expecting Captain Anton to be waiting for her. The secluded area was blessedly deserted as she lowered the stone panel into place and sprinkled sand to mask the door. She found Ramón in the park, twirling the reins of his black gelding and her gray mare in his hands. A relieved smile lit his face when he saw her.

"Another moment and I would have come to fetch you." Ramón pulled a strand of cobweb from her hair and examined her face. "What is amiss?"

Alecia frowned. "Nothing."

"You have the look of trouble on your face, Your Highness. If you don't wish to practise, we could go for a ride. The high meadow is nice in the early morning."

Alecia studied his earnest expression; his deep blue eyes could never conceal anything from her. Clad in a violet shirt under a dark gray tunic, with matching gray breeches and an ermine-trimmed black woollen cape, Ramón would turn heads in any of the kingdom's royal courts. Perhaps he should return to the King's court at Wildecoast, where he could make a suitable marriage. At least then he would not trouble her with his puppy love. But she would be lonely without him, and with whom would she practise archery and the sword? The crusty old weapons master was not half so much fun to tease as Ramón.

She hooked her bow and quiver over the saddle and pulled her reins from the his hand. "I've told you to call me Alecia when we're alone." She vaulted onto her horse's back. "Let us go."

Ramón climbed onto his gelding. "I will remember...Alecia." He heeled his horse forward, grinning.

Alecia followed, dismayed that she had given him hope that they could be more than friends. He was a dear chap and easy to be with, when he wasn't mooning around after her. She did not love him; moreover, she was destined for a marriage of convenience, though she longed to make a love match. Ramón deserved someone who could love him. She spurred her horse after her companion.

Alecia's mount slid to a halt in front of the palace stables, the gray mare half rearing at the abrupt change from gallop to standstill. She flashed Ramón a triumphant grin as he arrived moments later, pulling his horse up short of the flustered stableboy.

"You cheated," Ramón said. "I had to close the gate."

"It's my prerogative," Alecia said, laughing. The exhilaration of the race and her victory made her feel as if she could float away. She flung herself off the horse and handed the reins to the boy, who stood frowning. "We are sorry to have startled you, Billy," she said, handing him a silver penny.

The boy's eyes lit up. "It was nothing, Princess." The penny disappeared with lightning speed into his pocket.

"What brings you to the palace stables, Billy?" Alecia said. "Do you not serve in the smithy?"

"I did, Princess, but Captain Anton has taken me under his wing, so to speak." Billy adopted a worshipful expression. "He said I could care for his horse and he would train me in weapons."

Alecia frowned and looked at Ramón, whose face wore a scowl at the mention of Vard Anton. Her joyful mood vanished behind a dark cloud.

A deep voice sounded from behind them. "It'll be hard for me to keep my promise to the boy if he's trampled beneath the hoofs of your horses."

Alecia turned to find Vard Anton, resplendent in gray tunic and black leggings, lounging against a rain barrel. She swept her hair forward so it fell in soft waves against her cheeks and folded her cape over her arm. She shoved her bow and quiver at Ramón.

"I fear it is time for luncheon," she said. "If you will excuse me, I am expected at table." She tried to walk past but the captain's arm flashed out and blocked her way. The odour of musk, combined with something else she couldn't name, distracted her.

"I wish to know how you left the castle this morning without my seeing you," the captain asked, his voice low and angry. "Your father was worried, though somewhat reassured when he discovered that the squire had taken two horses from the stable." He looked toward Ramón who shuffled his feet.

Alecia's longbow fell from Ramón's arms and clattered on the stone of the stable yard.

Vard Anton's gaze snapped back to Alecia. "Is it your aim to make me appear incompetent, Princess?"

Alecia glared at Ramón clumsiness and he dropped the quiver in his attempt to retrieve her bow. She turned back to the captain, peering up at him through the strands of her hair. "I assure you it is not," she said. "Now let me pass."

His eyes narrowed and his voice dropped to a whisper she could barely hear over her thudding heart. "I've been given a task and I mean to see it through. No harm will come to you while you're in my care and I intend to see that you *are* in my care."

His blistering glare trapped her. She couldn't look away. Were his eyes even more gilded than usual? The scene around them receded until it was only Alecia, Vard Anton and this battle of wills. She felt herself slip under his dominion, his stormy golden gaze gentling her defiance like the firm hands of a trainer on the shoulder of a fractious filly. Finally she could stand it no longer and dropped her gaze. Damn, but that smarted!

He stepped away from her and strode toward the palace, his boots tapping an angry staccato on the paving. Alecia exhaled slowly, turning to find Ramón by her side.

"Are you well, Princess?" he asked quietly. "What did he say?"

"Nothing, Ramón," Alecia said, "I will just have to be more careful. Now hurry, Father will be waiting."

Alecia's heart and thoughts raced as she hurried to her room. She splashed cool water from a stone basin onto her cheeks, but no amount of washing could banish the embarrassing scene. That she should capitulate with just a look, albeit a long and smouldering look…He hadn't even touched her, thank the Goddess! She shook the memory of their meeting from her head and donned a pale gray dress with pearl buttons up the bodice and white lace at the high neck. Her fingers shook as she pulled her hair back in a simple twist and brushed some blush across her cheeks.

She joined Ramón outside the dining hall and they entered together. The prince was already there, seated at the head of the table and staring at the red wine in his crystal glass. He often had a glass in his hand these days.

"Hello, Father," Alecia said, with a small curtsy.

Ramón swept a deep bow. "Prince Zialni," he said, his voice a deal short of calm and assured.

The prince looked up at them and Alecia's heart sank. Her father was as angry as she had ever seen him. "You think me soft, Alecia," he said. "You think you can run around causing trouble wherever you please and I will turn a blind eye?"

She stiffened. Had her father discovered her part in the death of the mercenary? *No!* Surely he was just angry about this morning. "I do not try to cause trouble, Father."

"And you, Squire," the prince said, "should know better. Were you aware that I had placed the princess's safety into the hands of Captain Anton?"

"Yes, Your Highness," Ramón said. "I did not think —"

"You never think." Prince Zialni's voice cracked like a whip. "Arrangements have changed. You will no longer escort the princess as you once did. Do I make myself clear?"

Ramón went red but whether from anger or embarrassment Alecia could not tell. He cleared his throat. "I understand perfectly, Your Highness."

"You may eat with us. Be seated."

Alecia smiled at Ramón as he helped her to a chair opposite the prince at the end of the table. The squire took a seat halfway along on Alecia's left. She kept her eyes downcast, still frightened that her father had discovered her secrets. They ate in silence. Each second that passed tightened the band around Alecia's stomach. The faint scrape of metal utensils on china tormented her. Just when she could stand it no more, Ramón placed his knife and spoon on his plate, asked to be excused and left the room.

The squire was one of the few people she could talk to in the castle. He was like a brother, even if he didn't see it that way. She didn't want to see less of him, especially if it meant more of the captain's unnerving company.

The prince wiped his mouth on his napkin and cleared his throat. "Captain Anton went looking for you this morning but found you not in your room."

"Does he spy on me then?"

"He is watching over you, on my orders. If you leave the castle, you are to be in his company. If you are in the castle, you will let him know where you are at all times. For now, you may roam freely within these walls. If there is a repeat of this morning, when only Squire Ramón knew where you were, you will be confined to your chambers."

"I would be a virtual prisoner." Alecia's hands clutched the table edge. "What's next? The dungeon?"

"I will do whatever is required to ensure your safety. We must take steps to find you a husband so that you can give me a grandson to continue the Zialni line. He will be king one day."

"Even more good news," Alecia said, sarcasm thick in her tone.

"You've always known that an arranged union would be your lot, Alecia. Don't behave as though this is a punishment. We have responsibilities the common folk do not."

"I'm well aware of *my* responsibilities," she said. How could he talk about responsibilities when he sent mercenaries to collect taxes and innocent men died?

"What do you imply?" the prince said.

Alecia remained silent, berating herself for the outburst. If her father suspected the way she felt about the treatment of his people, she might fall under suspicion. Then the good people of Brightcastle would have no champion.

Prince Zialni stood. "You will give the kingdom an heir, and within the next year if I have my way."

"I don't even have a husband yet."

"I have someone in mind. It's a matter of making the marriage offer attractive."

"And when will you inform me of the identity of my husband-to-be?" Alecia asked.

"When he has agreed to the union."

Alecia rose, drawing the shreds of her dignity about her as best she could. "So, I'll be the last to know. Do you not care for my happiness?"

The prince raised his chin but his eyes didn't quite meet hers. "I care, Alecia, but will do whatever I must to ensure our family's claim to the throne of Thorius. Your feelings are secondary in the matter."

Alecia stared at her father. Where was the man who had tucked his little daughter into bed and taken her for pony rides? He had been the father who would always protect her, who could do no wrong. She fought tears, determined not to let him see how much he had hurt her. "I'll be in my chambers," she said.

"Alecia," Prince Zialni said, "do not disobey me." The words carried a definite threat. She swept her father a curtsy and left, slamming the door behind her.

Alecia returned to her room, schooling her steps to those of a princess, concentrating on her poise so that she could control the hurt and frustration building inside her. Once in her room she stood before the tapestry of Izebel, her shoulders slumped as she blinked away tears. Her heart told her to flee but her mind argued. It was too soon to disappear again.

She had to be crafty. Already Captain Anton might have searched her chambers and found the hidden passage. Though he would hesitate to cross her threshold, he would not rest until he had puzzled out her means of eluding him.

The escape route must be protected at all costs. Nothing her father had said at luncheon suggested that the secret passage had been discovered, but what if he and the captain already schemed to catch her out so that they could lock her up? No! She would not believe her father capable of that. What to do?

She paced the thick blue and gold carpet of her sitting room. Should she continue her plan of revenge against the mercenaries? Could she? Circumstances had altered dramatically since yesterday. She was now tied to Vard Anton, at least during daylight hours. Perhaps at night he would be less vigilant?

A tight band of fear clamped her chest at the thought of creeping about at night in the town, tracking down and disposing of armed mercenaries. She told herself it was just like the secret passage, only on a grander scale. She could do it if she had to. Hetty might help. The old woman hated the prince.

At the thought of her father, Alecia's composure crumbled and tears burned her eyes. He had treated his people harshly but she had never expected him to disregard her feelings. It must be the influence of Finus. The two were thicker than thieves.

White-hot anger flared in her chest, burning the fear away. Somehow, she would expose Finus and make him pay for his manipulation of the prince. She would find a way to avenge Jorge's death and stop this ridiculous arranged marriage. Alecia's fiery determination wavered as she faced her challenges.

In that moment, she had never felt so alone.

CHAPTER 4

SWEAT slid down Vard's chest and back as he fought off the onslaught from Ramón Zorba. They used practice swords but the weapons could still inflict damage. A cool corner of his mind wondered at the challenge from Ramón. The younger man handled the sword better than most but in the first moments of the match Vard had exposed serious flaws in the squire's technique.

Insolent pup! He thinks he can protect the princess! Savage anger rose within and Vard knew he had to put an end to this now before he lost control. Attacking with an aggressive flurry of blows, he cracked his opponent's defence. A savage strike to the side of the head knocked Ramón to the dirt, out cold. Vard paused long enough to hear Zorba's shallow breaths, to feel the thud of his heart, then threw down his sword and stalked away.

"See to him," he said to the weapons master, and left the practice yard.

Vard fought his temper as he sought the refuge of the castle park. It was really only a small wild garden but it would serve his purpose. He needed privacy to battle his demons. Many things angered him, including petty challenges from inferior warriors, but rage was his real enemy; had always been.

Pictures flashed into his mind unbidden; his cousin's body, bloodied, the flesh torn; warm muscle ripping under his teeth; blood spurting; a fresh grave; his father's sad face; a weeping mother.

Vard fought the surge of energy that carried him toward transformation. If he couldn't stop it, at least he could control the form. His breathing deepened as he clutched the stone at his throat.

He closed his eyes, sought the emptiness and then began to replace it with the image…

* * *

Alecia watched from her bedroom window as Vard Anton, naked to the waist, strode toward the entrance to the castle park. His right fist clenched and unclenched while the left gripped the curious amber stone. As she admired the hard muscles of his shoulders and stomach, a warm glow lit her lower abdomen. She didn't allow the pleasurable sensation to take hold, pushing it aside and instead concentrating on anger. The man below had no care for her happiness so why should she concern herself with what might have upset him?

He strode into the park and was lost from view. What business could he have in there? Was it solitude he sought? Peace? Perhaps he hunted the comfort of a woman. Alecia imagined his arms around her and jumped as she realized where her thoughts had carried her. *I must be true to Jorge's memory. I owe him that much and more.* She tried to distract herself with thoughts of Jorge but her eyes again found the captain. What had made him so angry?

As Alecia watched, a black and gold-banded hawk burst from the trees of the park and shot straight into the heavens until it was just a speck. That was odd. The local hawks were all brown and smaller. She struggled to keep the dot in focus but blinked and lost it. That bird had been magnificent. The thought that someone might capture the creature struck a chord of sorrow within her. Something that beautiful shouldn't be tamed.

Alecia pulled her gaze from the sky and her heart leaped at the sight of the same exotic bird perched on the roof of the stable. It stared at her, unblinking. The eyes appeared golden however it was impossible to be sure at this distance. She shivered and forced herself to look away and over to the park. When her eyes swept back to the stable roof, the hawk had vanished.

Alecia maintained her vigil at the window, hoping to catch another glimpse. The bird didn't reappear – and neither did the captain, even though she stood there until the light faded.

* * *

The banded hawk soared high above Brightcastle Town, the air currents ruffling his gold and black feathers. It had been too long. The sense of weightlessness was like no other experience, and something like joy filled the bird's brain. There was fear as well; fear at the fragility of life, especially for one such as him. A properly placed arrow could pluck his body from the sky and send it plummeting. Despite this, he descended from his lofty realm and alighted on a rooftop. His sharp eyes detected movement at one of the castle windows. A woman stood there. She was not beautiful, but so self-assured that it was a beauty in itself. They stared at each other for a time and the hawk again felt the fear of the unknown, of a fragile life, ever just one step away from death and oblivion. A small part of him longed for that oblivion. Longed for release from a life of constant battle, a battle that could be lessened by the shift; if only he weren't afraid of losing himself entirely.

The woman broke the contact and, as if released from a spell, the hawk took to the air, his strong wings taking him swiftly away from the castle and town. A juicy rabbit was his goal before the call of the body beckoned him back to reality…whatever that was.

* * *

Vard muttered to himself as he carried the dinner tray toward Princess Alecia's chambers. What was this anyway? Compulsion? Was she a witch? He seemed unable to act of his own volition. It was part of his Defender role that the vulnerable drew him when they needed help. That must be it. The princess needed him. She was in danger, or at least her father thought so.

He paused outside her room, his emotions still turbulent. The shift should have helped, but it hadn't. He took several deep breaths to calm his heart, which beat far quicker than it should, and forced his mind to focus on the job at hand. He would deliver the meal, and get out of there.

Vard knocked on the door. The princess opened it, drawing on a thick cream robe – but not before he glimpsed the pale blue nightgown that hugged her full breasts. Flaxen hair cascaded around her shoulders. He frowned at the tightening in his loins.

She drew herself up when she saw the expression on his face. "I hardly expected you to deliver my meal," she said, taking the tray and placing it on a small table just inside the door. She made no move to allow him entry.

His gaze swung past her into the room. Most young women would not have the lights this low. "I happened to overhear your request for a meal in your rooms and thought I could ensure that you were well at the same time." He turned back to her, his arousal deepening despite the layers that stood between them. He clutched the amber stone at his throat and her eyes followed as though mesmerized. No! It was not the princess but he who was hypnotized. *This woman intrigues me, but why?* He couldn't allow her to trap him. Despite his resolve, he stepped closer. She was not classically beautiful, but she radiated... something. Perhaps she *was* a witch; like the old woman of yesterday.

"Thank you for the meal. Don't let me keep you from your rest."

Her words broke the spell and Vard bowed to her, intending to depart, but some power held him in her presence. What did she want of him? Somehow he had to distract himself. "How did you do it, Princess?"

"I don't know what you mean." He heard tension in her voice.

"You managed to elude me this morning to go riding with Zorba."

"You don't guard me as closely as you may think. Perhaps you fell asleep."

Vard stepped over the threshold, forcing her to retreat. "I did *not* fall asleep!" His eyes searched her face, trying to find that which drew him against his will. Despite his enhanced sight, he simply couldn't see her well enough in this gloom. "You will *not* put yourself at risk again. I must accompany you each time you leave this castle."

"You and my father would have me live like a bird in a cage. I've been free, and I don't wish to have my wings clipped."

"It's no concern of mine what you wish, Princess," Vard said, distracted by the play of emotions over her features. In the half-dark, they were even more intriguing.

Her eyes sparked and narrowed as she took a step toward him, her hand raised to slap his face. A tingle ran through his body as his hand closed on her wrist. A blush appeared on her cheeks. Was it really anger she felt? Or something else?

Her lips parted slightly before pressing into a firm line. "Unhand me," she said, tugging at her trapped arm.

Before Vard could stop himself, his right arm looped around her waist inside the dressing gown and he yanked her to him, their faces only inches apart. Her rose perfume filled his nose and his heart beat a little faster as the heat of her body infused his. Her eyes widened and the muscles of her throat tightened as she swallowed, however Vard could discern no real fear. Was it bravery or was she simply too naïve to panic?

"You are as bad as he," she said, sounding breathless. Perhaps there was fear after all. Then she straightened her shoulders and her tone grew bolder. "I have a life to live and I don't see why you or my father should dictate to me."

Vard barely heard a word she said. He released her wrist and let his hand slide across the velvet of her skin. His left thumb massaged a lazy circle against the silken fabric at her waist and his eyes fell to her lips, slightly parted in her agitation. How he was drawn to them. Vard raised his eyes to Alecia's and again felt a stab of recognition. He tossed the thought aside, growling low in his throat. His head dipped, wanting to taste her mouth more than anything. Alecia's eyes widened a second before she shoved against his chest.

The spell was broken.

Vard stared, conscious of his racing heart. *Her* heart beat a quick staccato; again, there was something familiar in it. Perhaps they had met in a former life. Defenders could be reincarnated just as humans could. He swallowed hard, his gaze trapped by her hands as she smoothed her gown.

"I don't think my father had *that* in mind when he handed my safety to you." Her pupils were so huge that Vard could not have guessed the color of her eyes, even in good light. He drew a ragged breath.

"I'm sorry, Princess," Vard said, taking a backward step. "I don't know what came over me. I would appreciate it if you didn't mention my transgression to your father."

Alecia stared at him as if she couldn't believe what he said.

"If you've no further use for me," he said, "I'll leave you to your rest." When the princess remained silent, he bowed and pulled the door closed. Vard had no further awareness until he arrived back in his room, panting as if he'd run a mile.

He shut the door and slid to sit against the solid wood, his legs suddenly unable to hold him. *Forbidden fruit.* That must be the attraction. He loathed Prince Zialni – what better way to hurt the prince than to seduce his daughter? Vard shook his head. He deluded himself because it was easier than admitting the unthinkable. He was drawn to Alecia Zialni. She intrigued him, aroused him and, more than that, he admired her. Alecia had imprinted herself on him and her scent, her very self, had seeped into his being. No woman had ever had the potential to control him until now. He couldn't allow it to continue.

It was time to take action on the task that had brought him to Brightcastle. Kill the prince, and he could leave Brightcastle and the disturbing princess behind him.

Vard knelt in the shadows of the hallway, senses fixed on the sluggish heartbeat of the guard who sat slumped against the wall. *Not long now.* The beats slowed, the breaths coming so infrequently that on first inspection the unfortunate sentry would appear dead. He'd recover without adverse effects, the curious properties of the poison wiping all memory, timed to wear off before the next shift took over.

Vard glided from shadow to shadow up to the prince's door and entered without a sound. Gentle snores came from the bedchamber and Vard suppressed a small snort. This would be so easy: smother the prince in his sleep, make it appear he had died of natural causes; wait a respectable amount of time to allay suspicion, resign his commission after the funeral and leave Brightcastle forever.

Vard stood before the prince's bed, a thick pillow grasped before him, and pulled an absorbent cloth, soaked in surgeon's ether, from his pocket. First the rapid-acting sleeping sponge over the mouth and nose, then the pillow to cut off all air. There would be a short struggle but his strength was superior to Zialni's. He wouldn't fight long and Brightcastle would be free.

But what of the princess? Her brilliant smile shone in his memory and he shoved it from his thoughts. She would mourn and move on. Zialni had spoken of an arranged marriage and, according to law, Alecia's husband would rule until her first son was old enough to take over. Things were bound to improve in Brightcastle, and for Alecia as well.

Wouldn't they?

But he had seen triumph turn to tragedy more than once in the past. Had seen one tyrant deposed, only to watch as another took his place.

He raised the cloth, poised to clasp it over Zialni's face, ready to suffocate the life from another soul. *It was right!* Wasn't it? The wolf in him growled. He grasped the pillow and cloth in one hand and gripped the amber talisman at his throat, forcing his unease to quieten, his heart to slow, his tumbled thoughts to still.

Do it! Now! His limbs failed to move and Zialni's peaceful snores mocked his intent. The man deserved death. He had sent others to theirs. The deed rested well with his Defender goal to protect the innocent by whatever means.

Still, the fate of the princess nagged at him. He saw her face, tear-streaked, fixed on a coffin; met her accusing stare as she blamed him for the death. Something in Vard held him fast. This wasn't the time. He felt it so strongly it was like a voice in his head. *Go back.*

He left the prince's chamber, replacing the pillow as he went, the cloth tucked back in his tunic. The guard still slept, his breathing a little quicker than it had been. As Vard reached the castle entrance, he was gripped by a sudden urge to run. The creature within needed to be free, to escape the confines of man. He slipped through the front door, his mind on the wolf, human troubles dropping away to the call of the wild.

* * *

Alecia remained frozen for several minutes after the captain's departure. The heat of his skin had surely left its mark? She looked down at her right wrist but his fingers had left no brand. Had he been about to kiss her? She raised her fingers to her lips and shook her head. She was losing her wits over this man. *How dare he lay hands upon me* again*!* Alecia had to keep him at a distance for if he continued to behave like *that,* she might not have the strength to rebuff him. *Or the will.*

She clamped down on that thought, the flush of shame firing her cheeks. *Jorge does not deserve this!* No matter how quickly she banished them, memories of the "almost kiss" returned, along with the crush of his hard body against hers. Her reaction to him confused her. He should be nothing to her and yet from the very first contact there had been something... some connection between them that scared her. He stirred feelings she had never experienced with Jorge. Was it just that the captain was a tough man of action while Jorge had been a gentleman? The thought of her lost love and his devotion to her brought a heavy wash of remorse. *He is barely cold in the ground and here I am lusting over another!*

Alecia shook her head. Vard Anton could never be anything to her but a servant. He was years older than she and the wrong class. Her father would never let her marry a soldier. *Marriage!* Her heart lurched at the thought.

Deliberately, she turned her mind to her vendetta against the mercenaries. It would continue; it must. Jorge would not die unavenged. Her first attempt had almost led to disaster but in the end, the target had lain dead; if not by her hand. She could still do this, but it would take brains, not brawn. *Why did I not see that from the outset?*

Alecia pulled a parchment with the descriptions of the five mercenaries from her bedside drawer. The second on the list was the man already dead. First was a tall, thin man with narrow shoulders and eyes set close. The third was almost as tall and heavyset, with six earrings on each ear. He was bald but sported a bushy black beard. Fourth on the list was a man shorter than Alecia with close-cropped blond hair and a red gem set in the lobe of his left ear. Last of all came the one she had nicknamed "the Devil". Jorge's father had been eloquent in his description of this man: of average height with wild black hair balanced by a moustache and beard, cold green eyes and a cruel laugh. The Devil was the leader and his sword had cut down Jorge Andra as he tried to defend his parents. Well, he would soon discover how it felt to be the victim of cold steel.

But how to find these men? Her first assault had come on impulse. She had seen the five men enter the tavern and realized at once who they were. It was then a matter of waiting for one to come out. There had been no plan, and the aftermath had shown her the folly of that. She had heard The Dancing Lion referred to as a favorite watering hole for mercenaries. Would the killers continue to associate there or had her father ordered them to disperse? It was time to investigate.

Alecia shed her nightgown and donned a dark gray shirt and breeches, bundling her hair up under a tattered black cap. Then she pulled on the hood. She stuffed her nightgown with her spare blankets and placed her nightcap over the top. By candlelight, when the covers were pulled up, it would appear that she was still in her bed if anyone should check.

She retrieved five knives from a cavity inside the wood box and hid them about her person. A puff of breath snuffed the two candles by her bedside and she pulled the tapestry aside, whispering a prayer to Izebel to keep her safe. The stone door swung open with a low rumble and closed just as quietly. The trip to the trapdoor was uneventful and she soon found herself outside the castle walls.

Alecia paused in the stand of trees that hid the trapdoor. A three-quarter moon floated in the sky. She kept to the shadows as she made her way into town. The backstreets frequented by drunks, thieves and other unsavoury types were well known to her, but darkness made the narrow alleys forbidding. After half an hour of creeping through the putrid streets Alecia's teeth ached from the strain of avoiding notice. She stopped in an alley across from The Dancing Lion. Light blazed from the windows and the sounds of a woman singing a bawdy tune floated to her. The patrons were comfortable in their warm retreat and none ventured into the street.

Open slats on two windows at the front of the building, and one on either end, spilled lantern light into the night. Alecia cast her gaze around the streets and rooftops for signs of watchers but saw no movement. She took a deep breath and sprinted across the street to the alley beside the tavern, dropping beneath the windowsill. Her heart raced, her breath coming in gasps. She waited until her body settled, then peered above the sill.

The crowd was not large. The four men she wanted were seated around the room. Two talked together in a corner while the Devil and the blond man rested on a bench in front of the fire. Alecia flirted with the idea of boarding the place up and setting it on fire, before she caught herself. If she did that, she would be no better than the mercenaries or her father. She slumped back to the ground under the sill, her arms wrapped around herself. *What is happening to me?* First the incident yesterday when she nearly died, then the captain unnerving her and now she was contemplating killing innocents to attain her goal. She hugged herself tighter, shivers of panic sliding over her skull.

Massaging her temples with cold fingers, she took deep breaths to stem the rising dread. *I can do this.* As long as she remembered she acted for good, she could not fail. Tonight's task was to discover if the mercenaries still frequented the Lion. Now she could return to the castle to plan her attack.

As Alecia stood and made ready to leave, a commotion at the front door drew her attention. She peered around the corner of the building and saw the Devil push another patron onto the cobbles fronting the tavern. The big mercenary pulled the other man to his feet and turned him about. A sharp crack echoed up the street as the victim's neck snapped and Alecia's heart leapt so hard she gasped. Allowing the body to slide to the cobbles, the Devil turned.

Even in the dim light of the moon, the murderous glare of the big man heralded his intent. He started toward her, slowly, deliberately and, for crucial moments, Alecia froze. He was too big, too fierce! She would end her life in this dirty alley, and this man would add another murder to his crimes. *No!* She could not let that happen. Taking a deep breath, Alecia felt for the knives hidden about her person. Her chilled fingers fumbled the task. Finally, one came into her hand and she threw it. The mercenary flung his arm up and the blade glanced off his leather guard. *Harder, faster!* Her second knife wedged in his left shoulder.

He howled like a wounded animal. then pulled the blade from his flesh, tossed it aside and started toward her once again. Alecia yelped as her back bumped up against the side of the tailor's shop, and her attacker smiled. She fought the terror that clawed at her and inched along, her back scraping over the rough wooden boards. *A little more space is all I need. He's slow and I have the cunning of the fox.* The trouble was, Alecia's brave words didn't ring true in her heart. As she backed up, the Devil came on like a winter avalanche.

Another of her knives sprang into her left hand and she threw, gratified to strike the Devil's chest this time. He clutched at the hilt and a gobbet of blood spilled from his lips. Six strides separated her from the mercenary. Calm descended upon her as he closed the distance. She would not die a frightened mouse. Alecia found her last knife and threw it, the blade flying true to its target. Moments later, his huge hands closed on her shoulders, and his face loomed over hers as he bore her to the ground.

The air gushed from her lungs as his massive bulk settled. Alecia battled for breath and braced herself to fight those meaty fists, but the man did not move. The handle of her last knife protruded from the right side of his neck. Blood pumped onto her chest. *His blood.* The sticky warm liquid oozed onto the skin of her neck, and bile rushed up her throat. She pushed at the Devil's shoulders and kicked her feet under his legs. It was no use. She was pinned beneath this man mountain, barely able to draw breath. The body felt heavier by the second and the air she managed to suck in reeked of stale sweat, sour wine and the metallic stench of fresh blood. *How can this be happening again?* There would be no Captain Anton to save her this time. The best she could hope for was for one of the other patrons to find her when the tavern closed. Without warning, the dead weight shifted as the body rolled off her. She found herself staring up at Hetty.

Alecia rolled over onto her side, coughing. "What are you doing here?"

"I could ask you the same thing," the witch said. "Get up and come with me before that man's friends come looking."

Alecia scrambled to her feet and glanced at the tavern. The body of the other man still lay in the street. As her eyes swept across the Devil's still form, she spied two golden spots, like eyes, at the far end of the alley. A shiver of unease swept through her. "Hetty," she whispered. "Do you see that?"

"I see nothing but darkness," Hetty said.

The golden points had vanished.

Hetty tugged at her sleeve and Alecia jogged along behind the old woman, tensing each time they passed a side street, anticipating ambush from the mercenaries, or worse. She had not imagined those eyes. They gained Hetty's two-storey shack without incident and entered.

When the door closed behind her, Alecia turned to her friend. "I saw the glow of eyes at the end of the alley. What do you think it was?"

"Could have been anything, Princess. Might have been your imagination, after a shock like that. Now, tell me what you were about. Not on your vendetta again, are you?"

Alecia frowned. "I was just having a look. Then the Devil stormed out of the tavern and broke that man's neck. He saw me and I had to kill him." Dizziness swept over her and she staggered to a bench near the small fire in Hetty's sitting room, both arms wrapped across her body to halt the shudders. "I don't feel well."

Hetty stared for a moment and sighed. "Wait here, I'll get you some tea."

Alecia closed her eyes, praying that the room would stop spinning. *I've just killed the Devil! It was in self-defence but still I killed him. A* surge of nausea hit her and she breathed deeply to prevent her stomach from emptying. By the time she had battled down the sickness, Alecia was trembling so hard her teeth chattered. She couldn't give into this. She had to get back to the castle before word spread of murders in the town. In that moment, the thought of the trip back to the castle was too much to bear.

Hetty returned with a mug of steaming tea. "Drink this." She gave the brew a last stir.

Alecia took the tea and breathed deeply of its aroma. It smelled a little different. "What is it?"

"Plain tea with extra honey. Oh, and owl's blood for intelligence."

She stared at Hetty. "You jest."

"Do I? When I think of all those years I tried to teach you common sense… Do you believe you can even the score like a man would?"

"It is the only language they understand; violence and cruelty. Even my father."

"Especially your father, Princess."

"He too is a victim."

"Your father is no more a victim than that mercenary. He's the cause of all this strife. The sooner you realize that, the sooner you'll end the misery."

"You know nothing. Father is the victim of manipulation by his advisor."

"And happy to be manipulated."

Alecia stared at the witch, who glared right back. She couldn't accept Hetty's words but the stubborn set of the old woman's whiskery jaw told her arguing was pointless. "How can I deal with my father's mercenaries any other way?"

"It's your father who must be stopped. Permanently. You must discover the means. Violence against the mercenaries will only end in grief, and I can't bear to see you harmed." Hetty sat and placed her bony arm around Alecia's shoulders.

She looked at the old woman. "How did you move the mercenary? One kick should not have been able to budge him."

"I'm stronger than I appear," she said. "Are you injured?"

Alecia looked down at the blood congealing on her shirt and neck and shuddered. "No, just a little bruised." She took a sip of the sweet tea and found it was just an ordinary brew. Or was it? One could never tell with Hetty. She took another mouthful and warmth blossomed in her belly. Perhaps it would give her enough courage for the chore ahead. "I must go before I am missed."

"First, I wish to ask about the captain," Hetty said. "Rumor says he is now your protector."

Alecia frowned. News traveled fast. "Captain Anton has been given the task of ensuring my safety," she said, stiffly. Her eyes met Hetty's and Alecia lifted her chin.

"Not doing a very good job, is he?" Hetty said.

"He doesn't know what he has taken on." Alecia's voice rose. "If he thinks he can imprison me, make my life a misery in my own castle…"

"Does he know your secret?"

Alecia dropped her eyes and her voice. "No."

"You'll tell me if you need help. Tell old Hetty and she'll come to fetch you. You see if I don't."

"I wouldn't allow you to expose yourself so." Alecia straightened her shoulders and looked at the witch. "Whatever my father and the captain have planned for me… I will deal with it."

Hetty studied her for a long moment, her eyes full of pity, a frown deepening the creases in her brow. She opened her mouth but Alecia raised her hand. "Don't say it, Hetty. If you show me an ounce of sympathy, I'm not sure what I will do."

Hetty nodded. "You need to change those clothes. Come, I have a shirt and hood that will suffice."

CHAPTER 5

ALECIA left her clothes in the passage and stepped back through the hidden stone door into her chamber. Eerie shadows from her candle danced on the walls. It was all too easy to imagine hidden assassins in every corner. Her heart raced from the trip back to the castle. The night watch had been difficult to elude, and she had employed all her skills to navigate the streets without raising the alarm. She used the candle she held to light the two by her bed, then walked around the room, lighting every other candle she had. Three stout logs soon had the fire blazing, chasing the last of the night chill and the shadows away. The chores helped to ease her frayed nerves. Better that than think about what had transpired tonight.

All seemed to be in order in her rooms. Her bed was undisturbed. Had it been searched, the covers would have been hauled back. Alecia hid her remaining knives in the wood box then pulled on her nightgown. She jumped into bed and drew the covers over her head, determined not to think about the events of that night.

But as soon as Alecia stopped moving, a spasm struck her body and she trembled violently, teeth chattering. She curled into a tight ball around the frost in her core, hugging herself. Through the thin silk of her nightdress her fingers were icy and she couldn't feel her toes.

She closed her eyes and forced herself to take slow, deep breaths. The dead eyes of the Devil intruded; his blood again spilled across her chest in a warm, sticky puddle. Nausea swept through her and her eyes shot open. She pulled herself to the edge of the bed and vomited into her chamber pot until the violent spasms produced nothing. She was left weak, her stomach muscles sore.

Alecia's hands shook; hands that had taken the life of another being. The sharp scent of his blood stuck to her skin. She bounded from the bed to her washbowl and plunged her hands into the cold water, scrubbing them with the pumice stone until they were raw. The ritual of cleansing pushed her past the panic, but she could not hope to cleanse her soul in the same way. Somehow she would have to live with what she had done. Perhaps live with more than one death on her conscience.

Tears spilled down her cheeks. Some warm milk might help her sleep. Her mother had always said so. What would Princess Iona think of her daughter? Would she be proud? Or would her gracious, gentle mother condemn Alecia and her murderous plans? She raised her eyes to the large portrait of Iona that hung by her bed and sank to her hands and knees on the rug, hit by the memory of her mother's death.

She stood at the foot of the bed, her mother's rasping breath the only sound in the room. It took all her strength to look upon the still, withered form under the gold-embossed coverlet. Her father knelt by the bed, his hand clasping his wife's skeletal fingers, his lips moving in prayer. Alecia closed her eyes, trying to recall her mother's face as it had been: rosy-cheeked, smiling, beautiful, full of life. The longed-for image would not come.

"Alecia." It was not the sweet musical voice of yore but the whisper of death. "Come to me."

Alecia's heart thudded. She could hardly draw breath as her mother's faded gaze trapped her and pulled her closer.

"Alecia…I must leave you soon. I have not the strength to fight…" Iona's words were lost in a coughing fit.

"Gracious Mother," Alecia began, forcing her voice to be strong, "hold the hand of my mother and lead her through her trials to your reward. Look down on your daughter —"

"Alecia!"

Her head snapped up, the prayer lost in the sharpness of Princess Iona's voice.

"This is not the time for prayers. I don't have long."

Alecia leaned closer to catch the words as the momentary strength drained from her mother's voice.

"Daughter, I've loved you as I have loved no other. You are my joy and my future. Soon I must leave this life, but I will live on in you. Be brave and hold these words deep in your heart. Always be true to yourself and your beliefs. You hold within yourself so much that I have lost." She paused for breath and another coughing fit. Each bout left her paler, the shadows deeper beneath her eyes. "I know you will never fail as I have. Hold firm to what you know is true and always remember you are princess by privilege, not right. I love you, my darling."

"I love you, Mother." Tears cascaded down Alecia's cheeks. She could force no more words past the lump in her throat but grasped her mother's hand, willing strength to the frail body. As she watched, Princess Iona's eyes closed. Her chest no longer rose and fell with the agonising effort that Alecia had become used to. The skeletal fingers relaxed and Alecia knew her mother had left her.

Always be true to yourself and your beliefs. In the four years since Iona's death, those words had never been far from Alecia's thoughts. They motivated her to right the wrongs of her father; to save the condemned, to feed the hungry.

He had never been the same after the loss of his beloved wife. Was it grief, or the words Iona had spoken to Alecia that had wrought the change? Did he harbor resentment toward the daughter who had been his wife's greatest love?

Her eyes again sought those of the portrait and she thought she knew the reaction her mother would have had to tonight's events. It didn't matter. Her mother was not here to disapprove.

Holding onto the realisation that she could choose her own path, knowing no one alive could judge her more harshly than she herself would, Alecia drew her cream satin robe over her nightgown. The sight of her raw fingers as they tightened the sash was almost her undoing, but she pulled together the shards of her composure and stepped into the hall.

The flickering candle she held did little to dispel the dark. Anything could lurk in the shadows. Was the captain watching? She recalled the glowing eyes in the alley. Something had witnessed the death of the Devil – *the murder*. She had to face the reality that she had murdered the man. Revenge had drawn her to the inn and she was not sorry the mercenary was dead. She really was not.

Alecia steps stalled at the top of the stairs and she took another deep breath. Nothing lurked in the shadows. *I am safe.* The whisper of her bare feet on the stone was the only sound as she descended the staircase and crossed to the hall that led past the kitchen. It must be two or three in the morning by now.

A low moaning from further down the passageway made the hairs stand on the back of her neck. It must be some poor soul in the grip of a nightmare. She would just stoke the fire and warm her milk and be away before the owner of the voice woke. When she came level with the kitchen, her eyes were drawn to a door that stood ajar at the end of the hall.

She raised her candle. Deep gouges marred the wood of the outer panel of the door. She inched forward, the light flickering with the trembling of her hand. *Have I not had enough excitement for one evening?* She stifled an hysterical laugh.

Alecia drew level with the damaged door. The moaning had ceased but she was certain it had come from this room. She reached out and pushed the door with her fingertips. The barrier swung aside. Vard Anton sat on the floor, head resting in his hands. He wore not a stitch of clothing. It was as if all his soft edges had been scraped away by a sculptor's tool. Alecia could not move; could not breathe. All she could do was stare at lean buttocks, muscular thighs and calves, and a ridged stomach. And then he looked at her. *Goddess!* Alecia's gasp seemed loud in the quiet room. His eyes were no longer yellow-flecked but full gold that reflected the light of her candle.

She took a step backwards. He stood and pulled on snug-fitting breeches but not before Alecia glimpsed what lay within the curling dark hair of his lower abdomen. *I shouldn't be seeing him like this.* She took another backward step, ready to bolt.

"Princess." His voice held a faint tremor.

Alecia cleared her throat. "I should not be here," she said, unable to get the sight of his manhood from her thoughts. "I will leave you to… whatever it was you were doing."

He laughed. It had a bitter sound. "Perhaps that's best."

Alecia froze at the note of vulnerability and paused to study his face. "What is wrong?"

"It hits me sometimes."

"What hits you? Say something I can understand."

He reached out and drew her into the room. His skin burned against hers with such intensity that Alecia's question flew from her mind. All she could focus on was his heat and her frantic heart. He stared down at her as though trying to memorize every feature. Too late, Alecia remembered she had good reason to avoid his scrutiny. She dragged her gaze from his scorching eyes and looked instead at his chest. That didn't help at all. Her fingers itched to stroke the bronzed skin of his shoulders. She clenched her hands into fists at her bosom.

He placed a finger under her chin to raise her face. The gesture was one of gentleness but the heat had not left his gaze.

"Your eyes, Captain," she said, heart pounding.

"I won't hurt you." He stared at her then drew her to the lone chair in the room. "Sit and we'll talk."

Alecia sat, her knees shaking and breath short, as though she had run to Brightcastle Town and back.

"Am I not the last person you would wish to talk to?" She recalled their near kiss and something low in her abdomen stirred. "The role of protector has been forced on you. You cannot enjoy it."

He seemed to consider her words, and Alecia watched a myriad of feelings chase each other over his face, saw the torment he struggled to hide. His eyes burned into hers and she could not look away. I should not be here, she thought again.

He opened his mouth to speak and suddenly she feared to hear the misery of his gaze put into words.

"I must go." She rose and started for the door. The captain reached it first, his broad shoulders forming a barrier she could not slip past. He didn't touch her this time and the glow of his eyes had dimmed to the familiar specks. Had she imagined his earlier wildness? "I cannot stay here."

Vard Anton seemed not to hear her words. "Do you ever doubt yourself, even for a moment?"

The inquiry pulled her up short. She closed her eyes, remembering the events of the last two days. "Once I did not, but now ..." Alecia opened her eyes to find his intense gaze upon her. Why was he so desperate? "You can't mean to imply that you know doubt?"

For a brief instant, pain flared in the depths of his eyes but it was fleeting, replaced by the familiar granite stare. "Go."

Wherever the vulnerability had come from, it had been exchanged for the chill she knew well. The sudden transformation unnerved her. He stepped aside and Alecia fled through the doorway. She ran all the way to her room, without a backward glance, and was in her bed before she remembered the milk.

She sat, the thick covers bunched up around her chin, and recalled the exchange with the captain. What had happened to him? What had he wanted from her? Outside a cockerel crowed. Soon it would be light. She lay back on the pillows and closed her eyes. Her last thought was for a hard man with one very vulnerable, painful stain on his soul.

CHAPTER 6

VARD hadn't slept. He'd left his room at dawn in search of a distraction. Now he faced six of the more skilled swordsmen in the prince's personal guard. They stood warily, even though the practice swords would be unlikely to kill. Ramón was not among them. He was still abed after his wounding the day before. Vard quashed a flash of remorse over the injury. Zorba had put himself forward as the princess's protector despite errors in his technique. Better for him to discover them now than to lose his life or that of another through ignorance.

The swordsman with the flaming red hair launched an attack that had Vard on the back foot, scrambling to defend himself. He cursed his inattention. Or perhaps it was lack of sleep that betrayed him. The events of the night had struck his core, shaken the foundations of his identity and left him cowering like a wounded animal. Vard still couldn't believe he had so little control that he'd failed to carry out a simple task. And then to expose his anguish to the princess… Her pity wouldn't last long if she knew what he had attempted last evening. Transformation hadn't washed away his distress; had only added to it. This time, his fragile hold on humanity was more tenuous and even his Defender core was not sufficient to anchor him.

Vard fought off the onslaught and returned a flurry of blows, engaging the redhead as well as the black-bearded combatant to the right. There was no point in rehashing the night's adventures. He had to regain some control over his mind, and that meant calm concentration. That was why he had sought the practice field this morning. But the bearded man struck a chord in his wolf memory. Perception was altered when anything was viewed during a transformation. He saw flashes of another black-bearded man in combat with a youth, and then that same bearded man dead in the street. The eyes of the youth resonated with the human memory of his rescue of the lad and the chamber-pot incident.

Black-beard got inside his guard and scored a blow to Vard's ribs. The breath whooshed out of him. He forced more air back in so that he wouldn't go down. It was a trick that had saved him more than once. He scored an answering blow to the side of his opponent's head and black-beard dropped into the dirt. Dust rose as the five remaining shuffled backwards.

Vard didn't allow them the break they needed, dancing forward, his practice sword moving with blistering speed. Three of the soldiers lay groaning in the dirt before they had a chance to more than half raise their swords. The man with the flaming hair and the weapons master stepped apart to place their opponent at a disadvantage. Vard backed up, drawing on his ability to focus in two different directions as his opponents advanced from opposite sides. He scored a blow to the ribs of the weapons master and ducked under a savage slice from the redhead, then turned to find the redhead had launched another attack. The two met, their practice swords thwacking upright between them. The man was of matching height and strength but his breath had the sour smell of ale.

"What's your name, Sergeant?" Vard asked, through clenched teeth.

"Floyd," the redhead grunted. The man's hair was not his only flame-colored feature now.

"Your drinking will be the death of you." With those words, Vard hurled Floyd backwards and used his momentum to follow the man down, pinning his sword arm against the ground and ramming his own sword against the sergeant's throat. Floyd's eyes bulged with the pressure of the weapon against his gullet. "Think on what I've said." Vard pushed himself off Floyd, allowing a little more pressure to bear on the man's throat as he rose. The sound of coughing followed him as he left the practice ground.

Fools, he thought, but not more so than he. His destiny was to protect, but after last night, he was no longer sure what that meant. Oh yes, he'd been foolish indeed to take the steps that had brought him to this place. He shook his head. The distraction had worked for a time, long enough to bring his ragged emotions back under control. He was expected at breakfast.

When Vard entered the dining hall, Princess Alecia was already seated at the long table, halfway along the side that faced the servery. Her eyebrows rose and her gaze swept over him, lingering below his belt. He waited for her eyes to lift, smirking at the blush that stained her cheeks. He knew she recalled his undress of just a few hours before. But his amusement was short-lived. It wasn't just his skin he had laid bare. She had seen him at his most vulnerable, and it could not happen a second time. There was no telling what he might do if he lost control like that again.

He crossed to the servery and poured from a china teapot into a fragile cup, savouring a mouthful of the fragrant brew as he faced his charge. Her eyes had the dark smudge of fatigue beneath them. The niggling familiarity struck him again. "Did I frighten you last night, Princess?" He watched the delicate movement of her throat as she swallowed, and his traitorous heart skipped a beat.

"Startle, more like," she said. "You were not yourself... Are you... well...this morning?"

He took a deep breath and crossed to the table, disturbed by his reaction. He was vulnerable to her! That shouldn't surprise him after last night, but it did. Alecia was very much a part of his current dilemma, his lack of control. She was inextricably linked to this chain of events that pushed his restraint to the limit. The truthful answer to her question was "no".

"I'm recovered, Princess." He sat opposite her and piled potatoes and thick mutton on a slice of hot bread, glad that his voice gave no clue to his distress. Her presence tugged at him, made him want to bare his innermost thoughts. "Where's your father?"

She didn't answer for a moment. "He has been delayed. We are to start the meal without him. Why are you here?"

Faint stirrings of anger licked at his brain. How could she irritate and intrigue him at the same time? He took a deep slow breath, resolved to keep cool. "The prince requested my presence, Your Highness, otherwise you can be assured I would've eaten in the kitchen or with the men."

"I did not mean to offend." She examined his face, her head tilted to one side. Her scent carried a mixture of nervousness and intense curiosity, as though she were viewing an unfamiliar but dangerous beast. He supposed that described him well enough.

The silence between them lengthened, their eyes locked together. She gave a start and broke the contact when Prince Zialni stalked into the room. They both stood but the prince waved away their manners.

"Be seated," he said, then filled his plate and took his chair at the head of the table. "So many things to attend to and so little time." He looked at Vard. "Have you heard the news from the township?"

"No, Your Highness."

"More killings," Prince Zialni snapped. "In the same area as the first. There is foul murder at work here and I *will* get to the bottom of it."

Vard glanced at the princess. Her eyes were fixed on her plate. The fork in her hand trembled and a wave of her fear struck him hard. He had not thought her easily upset. "Perhaps we should discuss this alone, Your Highness," he said to the prince.

"Nonsense! Alecia has to understand the risks of her office. In the past, she has disregarded the need for security. It will do her good to see that even hardened mercenaries can be victims."

"Hardened mercenaries, Highness?" Vard said.

"The very same." Prince Zialni's brow creased. He did seem disturbed by the news. "Two bodies were discovered just a few hours ago outside The Dancing Lion. The men had ventured out of the establishment earlier in the evening and neither came back. One had his neck snapped and the other was covered in knife wounds."

Vard glanced at the princess to see how she took the news but her eyes remained on her plate, her knuckles white on the handle of her teacup.

"These two murders were the work of the same person, Highness?" Vard asked.

"I can't see how else you could interpret it though they were not both…" The prince's voice trailed off and he ran his hand across the stubble on his chin, his eyes narrowing. "Never mind; as you say, Captain, no need to discuss this in front of my daughter." The prince applied all his attention to scraping thick slabs of butter onto the warm bread.

Vard opened his senses to his employer and almost growled. No trace of inner turmoil radiated from the prince, nor scent of fear or bewilderment. He smelled of determination and cunning, but that was the essence of the prince, and there was nothing else to give a clue to what he'd been about to say. His words implied a deeper knowledge of the victims than he was willing to share.

Princess Alecia cleared her throat and rose from the table, dabbing her mouth with a snowy napkin. "Father, may I be excused from the table?"

Prince Zialni frowned, his dark eyes darting from his daughter to Vard. "Captain, I wish for you to take my daughter riding this morning. It will do her good to escape the sordid events of last night for a time. Select a safe path and be vigilant. You must be back before luncheon. Daughter, obey Captain Anton or there will be no more outings."

She frowned at her father. "I thought you said I was at risk? Would it not be safer to stay within the castle?" A pulse jumped in her throat and she wiped her hands on her skirts.

The prince's eyebrows rose. "Since when have you declined a ride in the country, Alecia? You will be perfectly safe with the captain at your side."

The princess stiffened, her teeth biting into her lower lip. "Very well, Father." She squared her shoulders and met her father's eyes. "If I may be excused, I shall change for the ride."

The prince nodded and Alecia avoided Vard's gaze as she curtsied, and swept from the room. She was clearly disturbed at the suggestion of a ride into the countryside. Vard had to agree. The last thing in the world he wished for at that moment was to be alone with the princess. Somehow, he must keep himself aloof, for that was the only way he could guard her safety and sort through his feelings for the intriguing Alecia Zialni.

CHAPTER 7

ALECIA stood in front of her oval mirror, fussing with the emerald silk riding dress. The color made her eyes appear blue, not the lilac she so desperately needed to hide. No matter how often she smoothed her brow the frown crept back. She had spied a puzzled expression on the captain's tanned face more than once, and what else could be the cause but a nagging familiarity? Eventually her protector would make the connection, and now she had another reason to avoid Vard Anton's company.

Whenever she thought of the encounter in his room, her heart fluttered as though a hand had reached into her chest and squeezed. The hard lines of his body came readily to mind, but it was not only his glorious form that trapped her thoughts. He suffered some affliction, and last night had needed the simple comfort of another human being. She had never imagined that the granite exterior of her fearless protector hid some dark pit of despair, but now she was certain it did.

Realising the bent of her thoughts, Alecia tried to concentrate on her attire. The skirt was divided for riding, though the garment was still cumbersome and nothing like she usually wore when she rode with Ramón. She felt like a traitor riding out with the captain, while Ramón lay abed. She had tried to visit him yesterday but he had sent her away.

Alecia sighed. The dress would have to do. Vard Anton was unlikely to recognize her as the lad who had attacked the mercenary. She pulled two strands of hair, from the elaborate pile on her head, so they curled past her ears. A little rouge, kohl eyeliner and Hetty's cherry lip balm completed the disguise. Her hand shook as she put the finishing touches to her face.

A knock at the door startled her and the eyeliner smudged her cheekbone. "For the love of the Goddess!"

She stalked to the door and opened it to find Vard Anton in the hallway.

"Excuse me, Princess," he said after a bow, "if you delay further, we won't be back for the midday meal."

Butterflies fluttered in Alecia's stomach at the sight of her escort dressed in his uniform. As she stared at his perfection, her heart threatened to pound its way through her ribs and she said the first thing that came to mind.

"I thought we could ride to the high meadow for some archery practice." Immediately she regretted the words, imagining Vard Anton's arms around her as he adjusted her grip on the longbow. It was too late to go back.

His gold-flecked, sea-green eyes made a slow inspection of her attire before trapping her gaze. "I'm at your command, Princess."

Mouth suddenly dry, Alecia strode over to the peg where her shortened longbow and quiver hung. She grabbed the items and hurried back to join him. "I'm ready," she said.

"I think not," he said and stepped closer. His white-gloved hand rose to her face and Alecia swallowed the gasp that sprang to her lips. The image of his naked body swamped her mind. *If he tries to kiss me again…* Vard's fingers cupped the side of her face and Alecia swayed toward him. His thumb brushed her cheekbone twice and then his hand was gone. She staggered, suddenly light-headed.

Vard steadied her, his hand at her elbow. "You had a smudge on your face, Princess," he said. "I couldn't allow you to appear in public less than perfect."

Alecia's heart leaped like a panicked toad. It was several moments before she could speak. "I'm hardly perfect," she said, "but thank you for your attentiveness." She swept past him and down the hall, concentrating very hard on maintaining a regal bearing, but determined to stay in front of her escort.

He caught her up in the entrance hall and offered his arm. She ignored it and gave him her bow and quiver instead. They walked thus to the stables where their horses stood, tails swishing at the flies. As Alecia marched to her dappled gray mare she studied the brown gelding that stood nearby, longbow and quiver slung on its saddle. Surely that could not be his first choice for a mount? She sprang to Silver's back, before the captain could assist her, and turned her horse to face the gate. Her companion raised his eyebrows.

"It was you who said we should not tarry, Captain, and it is you who are now delaying us."

His horse rolled its eyes and fidgeted as he mounted and slung the bows and quivers across his broad shoulders.

"What is your horse's name?" she asked, determined to stay on safe topics of conversation.

"Swift," he said. "He may not be much to look at, but he is deep of chest and sturdy of leg and has consented to carry me."

Alecia raised her brows at the last remark. Most horses consented to carry men; it was their purpose. The captain seemed to imply a contract between himself and Swift. She shook her head. "Let us go."

She watched her companion from the corner of her eye as the horses walked side by side out the palace gate. He rode well of course, with the balance of a natural athlete. The extra weapons didn't seem to impede his movement at all. Even one bow made it difficult for her, especially when speed was required. She would see how far his skill ran.

"A race," she said, and dug the tiny golden spurs at the heels of her boots into her mare's side. Silver leaped ahead, her nose outstretched as she galloped toward the high meadow and the archery range. Alecia's heart soared at the wind on her cheeks and the powerful movement of the horse beneath her. She glanced behind to see her protector several paces back and gaining. A brief glimpse of him was enough to show dark brows gathered and his mouth drawn into a tight line.

In seconds, Swift surged past and the captain tugged on the reins to shorten the gelding's stride. Vard Anton moved beautifully, his upper body so perfectly balanced that his shoulders barely moved. The weapons sat secure, never shifting to impede his horsemanship. His ability set her teeth on edge, even as he commanded her gaze. She was an excellent rider, but would never have Vard Anton's skill. The joy went out of the race and she pulled Silver to a walk.

The captain sensed the lack of pursuit and reined Swift in beside her. Alecia cast him furtive glances, bracing herself for his anger. She should have stayed with him, not galloped ahead, but for short moments she had been free. Her companion's mouth and stormy brows gradually relaxed. Finally he turned to her.

"You ride well," he said.

"For a woman."

"I didn't mean that."

Alecia frowned at his earnest expression. "Perhaps you did not. Where did you learn to ride like that? It's like you're part of the horse."

He shrugged. "I've spent many hours in the saddle."

Alecia studied Swift. The gelding still rolled its eyes, despite the obvious cooperation between rider and mount. What was the story behind that? Had he beaten the animal into submission? He didn't seem the type to take his anger out on a beast, but she didn't know him well enough to be sure.

She shifted her attention to the countryside around them. They rode through open forest on a broad trail that had once been a paved highway. In ancient times, this road had led to the thriving metropolis of Amitania on the other side of a low range of mountains. Now all that remained of the road was the occasional flattened stone glimpsed through foxtails and other weeds.

There were many stories about what had become of Amitania. Alecia favoured the tale of a greedy monarch who had bled his people dry, until the populace revolted and set the city afire. In the inferno and battle that followed, many had died. Some citizens of Brightcastle claimed to be descendants of those who fought the battle of Amitania. Perhaps she needed to remind her father of that story. There was no need for Brightcastle to suffer the same fate – and it would not while she had breath in her body.

As they rode, Alecia spoke of Amitania and the various theories relating to the fall of the city. He listened intently.

"You know," he said, "I like the one that tells how a powerful wizard ensorcelled the citizens of Amitania, so that they hoarded wealth and were overcome with hate and suspicion."

"I would not have taken you for a man who believed in fairy tales."

His eyes bored into hers. "There's much in the world that ordinary folk don't understand, Princess."

"I didn't say I was an unbeliever." Her comment seemed to silence her companion and his gaze strayed to the surrounding forest.

Alecia sighed. She couldn't relax in Vard Anton's presence. The muscles across her shoulders tightened as their journey continued. It seemed odd that her father should suggest an outing when he feared for her safety. That meant there must be another motive for the ride… but what? To get her out of the way? Or was the prince's purpose to remove Captain Anton from the castle?

Her mood darkened further and she made a conscious effort to shrug off thoughts of her father. Instead, Alecia focused on the warmth of the sun on her back and the sway of the horse beneath her. There had been few moments like this lately. Her eyes meandered over her surroundings. The yellow flowers of lady's fingers on their long stalks bordered the road and late hyacinths reared their violet-blue flowers amongst the trees. The rough bark of the oak made a stunning contrast with the smooth trunks of the beech, and all wore the striking golden hue of approaching winter. Fat squirrels skittered about, gathering their last acorns and chattering at the passers-by who dared disturb their foraging.

Vard Anton observed the forest too, but his gaze held the wary scrutiny of the guard. He reminded her of the spectacular black and gold-banded hawk that she had seen the day before, with his gilded eyes and piercing gaze.

"Can you not relax and enjoy the ride?"

He didn't take his eyes from the trees. "Your safety is my responsibility. What would I tell your father if bandits were to overwhelm us because I was gazing at the trees and the flowers?"

"You think there is danger in these woods?"

"There is danger everywhere, but no immediate threat that I can't handle."

"You are a confident man."

"I know my abilities, Princess."

That was all he said, and she found herself believing he could handle anything that presented itself, despite the vulnerability he had shown her last night.

Her silence attracted his attention.

"I've frightened you again. I'm sorry."

Alecia's face heated, remembering the last time he had shocked her. Now that his eyes were upon her, she found it impossible to banish the memories of his bare skin. They were almost at the perimeter of the forest. The archery field lay through the woods and over the hill. She booted her mare and Silver leaped ahead once more. Alecia didn't stop until she arrived at the practice range, panting almost as hard as her horse.

Captain Anton reined in beside her, his face like a statue carved from granite, except for a muscle that twitched along the line of his jaw. He dismounted, dropped their weapons into the grass of the meadow and stalked off with Swift to a tree, where he tied the gelding. Alecia bit her lip as she stared at his back. Had she pushed him too far this time?

Dismounting, Alecia led her mare to the same tree and tied her up without looking at the captain. She collected her yew bow from the pile and slung the quiver of arrows over her shoulder. The practice field was a grassy paddock 400 paces long and 200 paces wide, with mounds built at intervals down the length. The first mound with its practice target stood 100 paces away. There were other mounds at 150, 200, 250 and 300 paces.

At this time of day, with the sun over her right shoulder, the shooting should be easy. She pulled a sharpened practice arrow from her quiver and nocked it, sighting along the arrow all the way to the 150-pace target with its yellow bullseye. Her hand shook with the effort of pulling back the string. She breathed out, let her mind empty of everything except the target, and was gratified to see the arrow fly to the crimson ring, adjacent to the bullseye.

"Stop." Vard Anton's voice came from behind her.

Alecia lowered her bow and turned to him.

"First you gallop off without me and now you charge at this task like a rabid wolf. You make my job of caring for your safety difficult, to say the least."

"I'm simply having a little fun," she said, her own anger rising. "The Mother knows I've had little enough of that lately."

"From where I stand, your life seems full of it," he said, his voice harsh.

Alecia thought of the two dead mercenaries and Jorge. If only Vard Anton knew the truth. "You think that because my father is the prince I don't know hardship and discipline? Try being raised by servants who only care for you because they are paid to. Or consider my father's brand of discipline, which is to throw me in the dungeon if I don't obey him."

"Your father may be unfair in his dealings with his subjects, but you're his daughter. I don't believe he'd imprison you."

"He's my father and I love him, but I don't deceive myself. He would sell me off to the highest bidder if it were to his advantage."

He was silent for several minutes. "Perhaps you know some hardship in your own way, but you don't know discipline. I intend to teach you restraint and control before you break your neck or kill someone."

Alecia frowned. *Too late.* "Go ahead, let's see what you can teach me."

He reached for her bow, long fingers caressing the golden wood, and Alecia noted again the ridged scar on the back of his left hand. She didn't see it as a blemish. Fighting men carried many scars, all souvenirs of past battles. The captain would have other marks, tokens of his bravery. Once more the image of his naked body filled her mind and she imagined her hands on his skin, exploring, finding all those scars he must assuredly carry. Vard Anton's voice brought her wanton thoughts back to the present.

"Even this weapon proves my point," he said. "What I wouldn't have given for a weapon of this quality when I learned the bow."

"I'm no beginner." Alecia's heart raced and her face burned in the aftermath of her daydream, but the captain would only think her angry at his remark about her being a beginner. He would never guess the real cause of her agitation.

"We'll see." He reached behind her and pulled another arrow from her quiver. Alecia felt his breath against her cheek and stifled a gasp. He smirked as he nocked the arrow to the string. With one fluid motion, he marked the target and drew the string to his ear. The arrow thudded into the 150-pace target, dead centre.

Alecia stared at the target, determined to keep any expression from her face. "A good shot, Captain. Now try the 200-pace target."

He raised an eyebrow and handed her bow back, then picked up his weapon and quiver. An arrow was in his hand, nocked and released before Alecia realized. Her eyes sought the 200-pace target and she was unsurprised to see the bullseye hit once again. But it couldn't continue. She had never seen anyone hit the bullseye at 300 paces. Vard didn't pause. His arrows slammed into the bullseye at 250 paces and then, miraculously, at 300.

She stared. How was it possible? "That's one of the most extraordinary feats I've ever seen." A strong man could shoot the longbow that distance although not with the accuracy Vard Anton displayed.

"I'd like to say I could teach you to replicate the shot, Princess, but I fear you haven't the strength."

"Or the vision," Alecia murmured. "I can barely see that target, let alone hit it." What else was he capable of? The blood roared in her ears and for a moment Alecia feared she would swoon. She couldn't let him see how his abilities affected her. "Would you care to duplicate the feat?"

He grinned and proceeded to place four more arrows alongside the others. What manner of man was he?

"Now it's your turn, Princess."

Alecia wiped her hands on her skirts, then raised her bow. He handed her an arrow and their fingers brushed, the contact sending a tingle down her spine. She almost dropped the arrow but took herself in hand, angry at allowing him to put her off balance.

Vard Anton immediately moved alongside her as she took up her shooting stance. His hand brushed her right thigh and her heart almost leaped into her throat.

"I've found that to open your stance a little helps with balance," he said.

Alecia took a deep breath, willing her heart back to a normal pace, and moved her right foot further from her body. She raised the bow and nocked an arrow.

"Roll your elbow slightly out," he said.

She tried to comply but her companion had to run his hand down her arm to demonstrate the positioning. Her skin burned through the fine silk fabric of her sleeve. He felt as hot as the sun. She lifted her head to sight the target at 150 paces, and tried to make its golden centre the core of her concentration. It wasn't easy with the musky scent of her instructor clogging her wits. She drew back the string until it came level with her nose.

"You must draw it further for real distance." His hands were suddenly on her shoulders, his thumbs probing the muscles either side of her spine. "Use these muscles to help you draw the string."

Alecia's worst fear – that the archery would bring her into close physical contact with Vard Anton – had come to fruition. She told herself it was just a lesson. His touch meant nothing, but the excitement that darted through her body made it difficult to keep her focus.

The new technique allowed her to draw the string to her cheek. She sighted and loosed the arrow, maintaining her stance until the missile hit the target. This time she achieved the outer ring of the bullseye.

"Very good," he said. "An improvement on your first effort, which was ill-disciplined. Now, repeat the lesson until you land two dead centre."

He watched and corrected as Alecia sent arrow after arrow into the target. Finally, she had two she could claim. Her arms shook with fatigue.

They walked with their bows to the targets. The practice missiles were easy to pull from the boards, even for one of her puny strength. At the 300-pace target, their hands met on the last arrow. Alecia tried to release the missile but he held onto her fingers. Did he sense the energy between them? Her eyes rose to his and she found him staring down at her. Her stomach fluttered and her head spun. His arm came around her waist as her knees buckled.

"Princess …? Alecia?"

Her name on his lips sounded glorious, his voice rich with the promise of long kisses and strong arms and… What was wrong with her? The captain's splendid eyes were now full of concern. *Am I lying down? How did that happen?* Her quiver was uncomfortable against her back but she wouldn't let her gaze leave his.

"Alecia, talk to me."

His hand cupped her face and pulled her quiver out from under her. She relaxed against the warm grass, with a long sigh.

"Alecia!" He sounded worried now.

The spinning in Alecia's head slowed and she was able to focus on the whole of his face. Why was he upset? "What's wrong?"

"Thank the Goddess! You're back with me. I was stupid to push you so hard."

Alecia tried to sit up and he helped to prop her against the base of the target.

"I'll fetch some water," he said and went to rise.

"Do not leave me!" Alecia grabbed at his sleeve. "I'll be well in a moment and we can walk together to the horses."

Instead of rising, he sat beside her, leaned his head against the target and closed his eyes. After a moment he sighed and turned to her. "We'll travel back to Brightcastle when you're ready," he said, voice strained. Alecia was sure the gilt flecks of his irises were more pronounced. He stood up and strode away, tension in every movement.

"What is it, Captain? What has disconcerted you?" Should she mention this attraction between them? Could she make such a fool of herself? What if he didn't experience that zap every time their skins chanced to touch?

"Never mind, Princess."

Her heart fell at the formality. "Please call me Alecia, at least when we're alone."

He came to stand before her. "It wouldn't be proper. I must remember what stands between us." His eyes narrowed. "When you stare at me like that…"

Alecia dropped her eyes. *Goddess!* She had forgotten her fears of discovery in the excitement of the lesson. She couldn't afford to do that. Her heart pounded as he stood over her; she imagined him tortured with love for her that he could never express. What did he mean "I must remember what stands between us"?

He held out his hand and helped her to her feet. Alecia rested her hands on his chest to steady herself, just as she had that first day. His muscles tensed. Suddenly reckless, she twined her right arm around his neck and pressed the length of her body against him. Her eyes were very close to his lips; strong, sensuous lips that parted in a gasp. What would it be like to be kissed by such a man? Alecia raised her eyes to Vard's and let the yearning inside her show. All of a sudden, she didn't care if he knew her secret. His pupils became huge, the gold specks all but lost in the fullness of his desire. She pressed closer.

The war of emotions in Vard's face captivated her. Restraint fought arousal and ice battled fire. Fear of what might happen next trickled in past her fascination, but then his mouth descended on hers and every coherent thought evaporated. Walls of restraint within her, she hadn't known existed, crumbled, and she moved against his body as his mouth crushed hers. She curled both arms around his neck and pushed closer, delighted at the way their bodies fit.

He groaned as his arms wrapped around her, moving across her back and buttocks and finally up to caress the side of her breast. Now it was Alecia's turn to moan as desire surged through her, sweeping her along until she was suddenly afraid of losing control. She pulled away.

He stood gasping, his arms hanging at his sides. In a split second, the longing in his eyes turned to horror. "We shouldn't have done that," he said. "*I* shouldn't have done that. Please accept my apologies."

Alecia shivered, the intensity of the moment replaced with cold formality. "I'm a woman and you are a man. We did nothing wrong." Would her father see it that way? What if someone had seen them? Alecia looked around the meadow. Their horses swished their tails at the other end. It was high time they were on their way.

Vard gathered up the quivers. "Can you walk, Princess?"

"I'll be fine." She stalked ahead, managing to stay in front of him all the way to their mounts.

* * *

They rode home in silence. Vard didn't try to draw the princess into conversation. What could be said after what had transpired? He still reeled with shock, though he hoped he had disguised it from the princess. She had awoken something within him he hadn't thought he possessed. He wanted her like he'd never wanted any woman, but he couldn't have her. Was it her very unavailability that heated his blood? Perhaps the wise move would be to abandon his plan to kill Zialni, resign his commission and leave Brightcastle. Leave Alecia to the mercies of the prince and whomever he chose to marry her. There would be other women and other posts. The thought sent a pain through his chest.

From his position just to the rear, he admired the straight set of her shoulders and her poise. No matter her brave front, she couldn't hide her inner turmoil from him. Shock and confusion radiated from her, hitting him in waves that made him grit his teeth. He tried to block her distress from his senses, but the memory of her lips moving beneath his, of his body moulded to hers, aroused him again. What was it about her that stole his breath? He imagined her naked, their bodies entwined... *No!* He must stop this. Frustration and anger began to build. He had to contain them or risk the life of the woman he had sworn to protect.

"Princess," he said, "let's push on to the castle. Your father will be waiting. Don't allow your horse to run ahead." Vard kicked Swift into a canter and drew abreast of the princess. It would be another bad night tonight.

CHAPTER 8

ALECIA dismounted and handed her reins to Billy, the stableboy she had nearly run down the day before. That seemed a lifetime ago. On another day, she would have stopped to chat with the lad, but after her experience in the meadow she didn't tarry. She strode into the castle, leaving her bow and quiver with Vard. *Heavens!* When had he become Vard instead of Captain Anton? She knew exactly when!

By the time she reached the base of the broad staircase she was running, and careened into Ramón at the top of the stairs. He hit the wall with a grunt. Muttering her apologies she hurried on, anxious to be away from scrutiny lest her control slip. Her chamber door shut behind her with a bang and she leaned against it, pressure mounting behind her eyes.

She covered her face with her hands and groaned. Her world had been ripped apart, while Vard had been moved not a jot. Oh, she was foolish indeed to think she could steal a kiss from a man like that and suffer no consequences. *How little I know of men.* She had not expected…could not have known…In that one instant of madness, she had become a woman in every sense of the word. Her body longed for the hard strength of a man against it, and not just any man. She had never felt this desire for Jorge. Her feelings for her lost love seemed a water color compared to the vibrant oil masterpiece she had just experienced with Vard. Was this love?

No! She could not love a man she had known for so little time, and Vard had made it very clear he was not interested in her. Well, perhaps he had been distracted by the kiss; he had certainly seemed to enjoy it. Her heart raced anew at the memory of his hands on her breasts and back; the thrill, the heat, the hunger he had evoked within her. She recalled the hard passion of his lips and her stomach lurched, a fierce burning in her core reminding Alecia of what she had wanted to happen next. She would not have allowed it and neither, it seemed, would Vard. Next time, when she was not so caught by surprise…

There cannot be a next time! She pulled her hands from her face. Somehow she must rebuild her world around this abyss that had opened in its midst.

There was a knock at the door and she took a moment to compose herself before opening it. Ramón stood without. The large purple bump on his left temple loaned him an air of danger.

"I have your bow and quiver, Princess," he said, eyes concerned. "What has he done to you?"

"I don't know what you mean."

Ramón took a step forward and Alecia brought her hands up to fend him off. He stared into her eyes then reached out and gripped her fingers. "You can tell me. We're friends, are we not?"

Alecia's eyes dropped. She needed to talk about her feelings for Vard, but not with Ramón. He could never give her the advice she required and would be even more hurt than he was already.

"Alecia," Ramon said, his fingers tightening on hers, "you know I care for you. I can't stand by and watch that man hurt you. Stay away from him. You heard what he did to me." His hand rose to his head and he winced.

Alecia bristled. "You say we are friends and yet you refused to see me when I came to sit at your bedside yesterday."

"I was angry, but I am no longer, at least not with you. Captain Vard Anton I would run through in a moment if I had the chance."

"Please don't try, Ramón. I couldn't bear it if anything happened to you."

Ramón's blue gaze met hers and Alecia's heart ached at the hope shining there. "I could make you happy." He raised her hand to his mouth and kissed her fingers. "Do you think His Highness would consider me as a suitor?"

Alecia drew her fingers from his grasp. "I don't know my father's mind. All I know is that he plans an arranged marriage for me and that he wishes an heir within the year."

Ramón gasped. "That doesn't leave much time for courting."

"I'm sure he has someone in mind." Alecia stepped back to put more distance between them. She had to be strong; talk of her impending marriage would only weaken her further, especially with Vard's embrace fresh in her mind. "We must remain friends only."

"Then that must be enough," he said. "Be on your guard against Anton. I've seen the looks he gives you and it puts me in mind of a lion stalking a gazelle. Don't trust him."

Alecia sighed. "He's my protector, Ramón. Are you certain your concern is not merely jealousy that he may spend time with me and you cannot?"

Ramón raised his chin, his eyes more serious than she had yet seen them. Alecia caught a glimpse of the man he would one day become. Perhaps a man that Vard could respect. "I've seen his face when he observes you. I know what it means."

"Thank you for the warning." She raised her hand to take the weapons from him. "If you will excuse me?"

Ramón opened his mouth but Alecia forestalled him with a shake of her head. He bowed and handed her the bow and quiver then strode off down the hallway. She closed the door behind him, her mind a flurry of thoughts and impressions as she gazed at the weapons in her hands. The last few days had turned her world on its head. Who was she? Girl or woman, victim or avenger, pawn or...? How could she judge the way forward unless she was honest with herself?

As Alecia changed clothes for luncheon, she reviewed the facts. Jorge was dead and someone must pay for his murder. Would it be the remaining mercenaries, her father or Finus? She had killed a man, albeit in self-defence. Could she go on killing to avenge her first love, a man as gentle as a lamb, who had gone to the slaughter to defend his parents? Vard had kissed her, awakening desire for the first time, showing her how wonderful it could be between a man and a woman. What she had felt for Jorge was not true love or passion. Could she countenance a marriage of convenience, knowing what she might be giving up?

Somehow it was all interlinked. Jorge, her father, Finus, the mercenaries, Vard and the events of the past days and months were coalescing to forge Alecia into the woman she needed to be. She shook her head. What if she was wrong and it was not all some grand plan of the Mother's?

Alecia finished dressing and stood before the portrait of *her* mother. As she gazed at beautiful Princess Iona, Alecia's disquiet vanished. She was the Princess Alecia Zialni. Her father may have the power here, but she too had power and she would not allow anyone to take it away. She would exact revenge for Jorge's murder and not allow her father or Vard or even Ramón to dictate how her life would be lived.

* * *

Vard sat on the bench in the kitchen and read the message on the tattered parchment for what seemed the hundredth time. A pretty serving girl, blonde curls peeking from beneath a white muslin cap, sauntered up to him, with his plate of mutton and vegetables. When he failed to take the plate from her, she laid it on the bench and sat beside him, her thigh pressed against his. He crumpled the paper, threw it into the fire and watched the flames eat the note.

"I could help you forget whatever's in that note, Captain," she said. Her hand caressed the side of his jaw.

The girl was more than inviting, and at one time he would've taken her up on her offer. "I don't think so, Miss."

"Oh, I'm no 'Miss', Captain. You can call me Larissa, or Larry if you like. I know a nice warm hayloft where we won't be disturbed." She leaned closer, her minty breath swirling up Vard's nostrils. His eyes fell to her mouth. It would be easy to allow this distraction and would hurt no one. Well, most likely it would hurt no one. In his current state there was a chance that he could lose control and then Larissa would be at risk. He couldn't allow that and still call himself a protector of the innocent, a Defender. He sighed and stood up. "I must decline, Larissa."

As the kitchen girl stood, her arm curled around his waist and she pulled his body against hers. "There's not too many as would turn down Larissa, Captain," she said, her tongue licking pink lips.

It was almost Vard's undoing. Why should he not have some fun? A vision of torn flesh ripped through his mind and he pushed the buxom maid away.

"No!" he said, unable to keep the growl from his voice. He stalked from the kitchen and down the hall to his room, slamming the door behind him. As he lay on his bed, staring at the exposed beams of the ceiling, arousal surged through him. *Why can I not control my urges?* His mind tumbled through the events of the past three days, replaying and sorting the scenes.

The clarity he usually brought to his problems eluded him, but one thing was clear. Princess Alecia Zialni was the source of much of his consternation. Well, perhaps that was unfair. She disturbed him, attracted him, infuriated him and aroused him, but it was hardly her fault that he'd been thrust into the role of her protector.

Huh! If the prince suspected for one minute the raging struggle within his daughter's guardian, he'd kill Vard and stick his head on the wall of the smoking room. Vard growled as he pictured his head alongside that of the grizzled old wolf that already adorned the prince's retreat. Unbidden, the death of the black-bearded mercenary flashed into his mind, though what his wolf-self remembered was the blood and the man-smell of the unfortunate fighter. Vard retained enough to understand that the lad had killed the mercenary, and that the young man had again been aided by the witch. But why were mercenaries being targeted?

The old woman had told him nothing last evening, just as on their first meeting. She could be a force for good or evil, just as he could. Hell, sometimes the boundaries were blurred when it came to taking sides. More importantly, did she know what he was? He couldn't afford for her to expose him. He had a job to do, and the note had urged him to move ahead with all speed on the mission that had brought him to Brightcastle.

Vard swore and rose from the bed, pacing from one side of the room to the other. He could see no immediate end to his quandary. Something stayed his hand against Zialni. Was it his concern for Alecia or the even deeper instincts of the Defender? Had he got it wrong when he accepted this mission? What would happen to the princess if he killed Zialni? Alecia was not the heir to the throne. If Zialni were to die, Alecia's cousin Piotr would take his place – and where would that leave her? Was that the whole point of this task, to move Piotr one step closer to the throne?

It was Vard's sworn duty to protect the princess, and the responsibility lay heavily upon him. Honor and his very essence might prevent him from leaving her, prevent him from destroying her father; would they keep her safe from *him*? From a transformation he couldn't control? He punched the wall, plaster crumbling to the stone floor. *I need to act!* A bold plan would carry him forward from this quagmire, but might it also destroy him…or the princess?

CHAPTER 9

A LECIA'S resolve to act, to be her own woman, faltered before it could solidify. For three days her waking dreams and nightmares were plagued by visions of the Devil, as he bled all over her and breathed his last. Her appetite dwindled to portions that would not have kept a sparrow from hunger and she kept to her room, though that had more to do with her fear of confronting a certain man.

When her mind didn't torture her with visions of the dead mercenary, it haunted her with the lips and hands of Vard Anton. Her moods alternated between frantic weeping and furious curses at the injustice of it all. How could he awaken her womanhood and then reject her? Had their stolen moment meant nothing to him? Did he not know that she woke in the night with the heat of his hands on her body, certain he was in her bed? She did not want to hear the voice of common sense that told her that a mere kiss had no power to change the life of a man such as Vard Anton.

Her attempts to distract herself with plans for revenge against the remaining mercenaries resulted in further frustration. The self-appointed champion of her people could not even set foot outside her apartments. She was her worst nightmare come to life – a good-for-nothing princess.

Prince Zialni had visited her the previous day. He seemed content to think her withdrawal was a result of their discussion regarding her upcoming betrothal. On that topic he had no more to add. Alecia was certain she would know the identity of her bridegroom before long. She dreaded the day.

Vard appeared to welcome the respite from her company. She could see the weapons practice ground from her chamber windows and his figure was a regular sight. She was exhausted just watching him. Did the other combatants tire of being beaten on a twice daily basis? There was a sullen set to their shoulders as they faced up to him. If Vard did not find some other activity to occupy himself soon, there would be trouble. In her sillier moments, she fantasized that the purpose of his weapons practice was to distract himself from thoughts of her.

On the afternoon of the third day after the kiss, Alecia sat on her sill as Vard stalked toward the stables. Eyes glued to his form like a starving man would view a pie on a window ledge, her fingers itched to caress the hard muscles of his chest. As if he knew someone observed him, he raised his head and their eyes met. He stopped and Alecia held her breath, her heart slowing, blood roaring in her ears.

He frowned and strode past the front gates and into the garden, stopping abruptly to retrieve something from the base of a huge old oak. Alecia's breath caught in her throat. *It's a baby hawk!* Vard tucked the tiny bird into his tunic and began to climb. Alecia clutched the windowsill, hardly daring to breathe as Vard climbed higher and higher. He never slipped, never hesitated for a hand or foothold. Just short of the top branches, a misshapen pile of sticks blocked his way, and Vard gently placed the baby hawk beside its two siblings.

Alecia's knees suddenly felt weak and she slumped against the windowsill, heart pounding as if *she* had climbed the tree. Though he had made the task appear simple, she knew from painful experience that it was not. And all for a baby hawk… When she sought the nest again, Vard was gone. Abruptly, her world seemed duller.

Alecia snorted and began pacing the room. What ailed her? She hungered for a glimpse of the man but feared to come into his presence. *It makes no sense.* Perhaps she should talk to him – her stomach lurched at the thought – so that they might clear the air. It could not be quite so bad to confront Vard as she imagined. *What if it's worse?*

There was a knock at the door and Millie entered. She carried an embossed envelope on a silver tray.

"Excuse me, Princess. I have an invitation from His Highness."

Alecia's hand shook as she picked up the missive. "Does my father wish for a reply, Millie?"

"He said to tell you that your presence was *required*, Princess. He didn't mention a reply."

Alecia flinched at the prince's choice of words. Now she was even more nervous of its contents. "That will be all, Millie."

The maid dropped a curtsy and left.

Alecia ran her fingers over her name, written in flowing silver script on the envelope. Why had her father not spoken of this yesterday? Were the contents so dire that he couldn't talk to her face to face on the subject? She removed the stiff parchment from the envelope and took a deep breath before unfolding it.

Princess Alecia Zialni's presence is requested at a ball to honor His Majesty, King Beniel, to be held in Brightcastle audience hall on the morrow at dusk. The princess is to be accompanied by Captain Vard Anton on this auspicious occasion.

The note was signed "His Highness, Prince Jiseve Uinnis Zialni, heir to the throne of Thorius".

The paper dropped onto the amethyst and gold-patterned rug that lay between the bed and the fireplace. Her escort would be Vard! She would have to dance the first and last dances with him as tradition dictated. Perhaps there would be other dances as well. Alecia rubbed her stomach in a vain attempt to quiet the butterflies as she anticipated the strength of his arms, hard body moulded to hers, his lips… Heat suffused her. *Do I have the courage to look him in the eyes after he rejected me so completely?* There was nothing for it but to bear up as best she could.

She focused on the other news contained within the missive. King Beniel was to visit. Alecia had only seen him twice in the past six years, most recently at her mother's funeral and before that at her debut when she was eighteen. She and her parents and Squire Jorge had traveled to the King's seat at Wildecoast where she had been presented at court with other royal young ladies. Jorge was her escort on that occasion and she smiled as she remembered his nerves. She, of course, had not been at all uneasy. After all, coming-of-age ceremonies were only important to young women who had nothing better to do than pose and preen themselves before the men of the court.

A niggling worry dragged her back to the present. The king was to attend a ball here tomorrow – and she was just learning of it. What did it mean? Nothing good, Alecia was sure. True, it paid to keep state visits a secret, even from those closest to the throne, but this was ludicrous. How long had it been planned?

Alecia smoothed her skirt where sweaty fingers had gripped the fabric moments before. She contemplated the guest list. Ramón was certain to attend. There were not so many nobles in Brightcastle that her father could afford to leave the squire off the invitation list. Perhaps the prince would need to invite several of the more influential merchants and the heads of the guilds as well. And King Beniel would bring along his own contingent of lords and ladies.

Lord Finus would be there, of course. Alecia's lip curled at the thought of her father's advisor. After she had removed the mercenaries, she would dispose of the manipulator. Now *there* was the man Ramón should be warning her against. She shuddered. Finus's eyes were always cold and cunning when they rested upon her, as if the man calculated how Alecia could best be used in his schemes.

She forced the lord from her thoughts and removed a dress wrapped in a silk sheet from her wardrobe. It had been her coming-of-age gown, and wearing it would honor the King. He would remember the gown, or someone would mention its significance. She sighed. If only her father were more like dear Uncle Beniel.

Alecia laid the bundle on her bed and removed the sheet. The cream satin gown, with pearl beading and gold thread embroidery on the bodice, was even more beautiful than she remembered. She retrieved the cream satin slippers from the chest at the end of her bed and opened her jewellery box. The amethyst necklace and earrings that had belonged to her mother would be perfect. She would leave her fingers bare, as her mother had always done, no matter how much the prince wished for her hands to be cluttered with gaudy baubles.

As for Prince Zialni, Alecia could imagine his excitement as he prepared for the occasion of the King's visit. How had he kept the event from Millie's ears? Surely he had an army of servants working on the audience hall right at this minute. If this had been an event long in the planning, the hall might have been readied quietly and with little fuss. If Alecia had not hidden away in her chambers the past three days, she might know more of the goings-on in the castle.

But all this preoccupation with the king and her gown and how long the event had been planned was merely a distraction to avoid thinking about the serious problem the ball posed. Her escort for the evening was the man she had avoided for the last three days.

A sharp knock at the door made Alecia jump, but it was only Millie who bustled back into the room.

"Princess, I've come to see if there's anything you need prepared for the ball." She gazed upon the cream dress. "Is that the gown you'll wear?"

Alecia laid the amethyst necklace beside the ball gown. "Yes. It will need a steam."

Millie rewrapped the garment and lifted it from the bed, taking the slippers as well. "I must go and deliver the captain's dress uniform." Her eyes unfocused as if she saw something Alecia did not. "Now there's a man to marvel at. I hear tell he can't be beaten at arms. The men are angry but you won't hear me say anything against him, not when he's taken young Billy under his wing."

The maid bobbed a curtsy and left. Alecia barely noticed so distracted was she by Millie's words. Vard Anton was an enigma, a hard fighting man with hidden demons, who still cared for the least fortunate creatures in his domain. How was she to prepare for an entire night in his company? And how could she possibly resist the lure of this unfathomable man?

* * *

Vard's boots crunched on the autumn leaves as he leaped the last few paces to the ground. The reality of his current dilemma came crashing back in, as the Defender drive to protect left him. His best-laid plans to avoid Alecia had not been sufficient to evade escorting her tomorrow evening. He was trapped but didn't need to be so, if only he could deal with Zialni. The man was like a wound that wouldn't heal, sapping the strength from good people who deserved better. Vard couldn't even take the simple steps that would rid Brightcastle of the tyrant. The prince should now lay dead after a hunting accident, but Vard's fingers had frozen on the arrow, doubt over his purpose crippling his resolve.

As he sat upon a stone bench under the huge oak tree, frustration boiled up within him. He pushed his face into his hands while images of sharp fangs tearing flesh bombarded him. Never before had he had so little control: of himself, of his life and especially of his emotions. He spent too many of his waking hours fighting the transformation. Twice he'd had to pull himself back from the brink, forcing himself into the hawk, a shape he could control and one from which he knew he could return.

The last two evenings, he'd dreamed of transformation, waking in a cold sweat moments before the change. He had no idea what would happen if the change were completed in a dream, but he feared it could lead to a waking transformation that would be impossible to reverse.

He slammed his fist into the stone of the bench and watched as the edge crumbled under the force. His body was changing. He shouldn't be strong enough to cause such damage. Fear lay like a cold stone in his stomach. He had to find another Defender, someone who could give him the guidance he needed. But he couldn't afford to leave Brightcastle yet, though that would be much the safest course for himself and those around him.

Vard's thoughts turned again to Alecia. He hadn't seen the princess face to face for three days – except just now, as she stared at him from her window. She had hidden herself away since that day in the meadow and he couldn't blame her. At least she'd be safe in her chambers, but the niggling worry over how she had eluded him the morning of her ride with Zorba persisted. Now, the advent of the ball presented further difficulties. He must put this obsession with her body and her lips aside. At least in public, she'd be protected from him.

He rubbed the stone that lay on the leather thong around his neck. The solidity of the talisman beneath his fingers grounded him. His breathing slowed and he let his fingers drop back to the bench. He had work to do in preparation for the King's visit and not much time to complete it. Security arrangements would be a welcome distraction from his troubles.

CHAPTER 10

THE following morning dawned bright and clear. Alecia breakfasted in her chambers, the drapes drawn back to reveal Brightcastle town and the Southern Alps. Her father had crossed the mountains in his youth and often spoke of the marvellous cities and people from far off. The stories had ended with the death of Princess Iona. Smiles had given way to dark moods, benevolence to hoarding and an obsession with the trappings of his office.

Why did his loss mean suffering for the people of Brightcastle? Were Alecia's efforts to restore the balance of right and wrong having the desired effect? Should she be trying to influence her father and counter the evil advice of Lord Finus, rather than rescuing individuals and exacting revenge? Would the prince listen to her? Probably not. His entire focus seemed to be securing the throne for his line, and that meant a husband for Alecia and male children as soon as possible.

The king had so far produced no heirs, and royal watchers muttered about the queen's miscarriages. Alecia knew how her aunt longed for children and was only too well aware that a son for the king would make her father's need for an heir less pressing. Perhaps this trip would be the tonic the queen craved and there would be good news in the spring. It would not come soon enough to save Alecia.

She sighed and dropped her napkin on her plate. Those were problems for another day. It was time to dress so that she could greet King Beniel and Queen Adriana on their arrival. It would be good to see them again.

* * *

Vard buttoned his shirt and met his eyes in the mirror. His black dress uniform was spotless, as were his boots. The sword at his right hip was freshly sharpened and the silver tassels on the scabbard washed and combed. The prince would not find fault and neither would Alecia.

He frowned at the thought. Alecia's opinion of him wasn't important. Her safety was the only thing that mattered. The prince had been adamant about that, declaring that Vard must not let the princess from his sight. The man was paranoid and possibly mad. That would explain many of his actions.

Vard's frown deepened and he turned from the mirror in disgust. He had been responsible for all the security arrangements for the King's visit until he had reported to the prince this morning. Now the security of the king rested in Lord Finus's hands. Vard didn't understand the reason for the change, and anything he didn't understand made him nervous. Vard had met Finus's type before and they couldn't be trusted.

Alecia's safety remained with Vard and that made him edgy for several reasons, not the least of which was the kiss they had shared. His mind wouldn't leave it alone and his treacherous body wanted more. Perhaps the princess would be better off escorted by Finus. He snarled at the thought of the lord's hands on Alecia and gripped the stone until his heart slowed to its normal rhythm.

The king would be arriving soon. Time to take one more ride along the route the monarch would travel, just to be certain all was in order.

* * *

Alecia sighed as Vard cantered his brown gelding back through the main entrance. He did look striking in his uniform, dark hair curling over his collar and white gloves gripping the reins with practised ease. Even on the nondescript gelding, he had a presence that could not be disregarded. A gorgeous black destrier or a dappled gray charger would have suited his nature so much better. Her father had many horses, more than he could ever hope to ride. Perhaps she could convince him to give Vard a mount that suited his station.

She turned back to the gilt-edged full-length mirror that hung on the wall beside the window. The striking cobalt-blue satin gown was embellished with silver embroidery on the strapless bodice and on the hem of the organza overskirt. The lacing at the back accentuated her small waist, and the color made her eyes appear blue. She reached for the silver tiara and placed it in her hair, then donned the sapphire necklace and earrings that her mother had always said were her favorite adornment. It seemed to Alecia that jewellery was the only item of her mother's that she had to remember her by. Still, it was an enduring monument to the woman who had left her life much too soon. She pushed the sad thoughts from her mind and turned her attention to her makeup.

As she applied the last stroke of blusher to her cheeks, there was a knock. She opened the door to Vard. Her heart raced as his eyes ran over her finery and then rose to meet hers.

"It seems long since I last saw you, Princess." His voice sent frissons of excitement along her nerves. Alecia wished he would say her name again, as he had the day in the meadow. *I was wise to avoid him.*

She wrapped herself in aloofness. "I've been busy. I thought you would be glad to have the duty of my safety off your hands."

A spasm crossed his face that Alecia couldn't interpret. Was it anger, disquiet? Perhaps some of each? The steely mask slipped back into place.

"Your safety is always my duty, Princess, whether I spend time in your company or not. I'm here to escort you to greet His Majesty King Beniel, and this evening you'll accompany me to the Grand Ball." He stepped aside, his hands tightening into fists for a moment. *What has unnerved him?*

Alecia joined him in the hall. She looped her arm through his, admiring the stony muscles of his forearm.

He removed her arm and placed her fingers there instead. "Best to follow protocol, Princess. You wouldn't want anyone to assume we are betrothed."

Her stomach flipped at his words and she snatched her hand away, intent on adjusting her dress one last time. What must he think of her? She had circled her arm through his in the intimate style of lovers, without thinking. He waited for her to complete her fussing and placed her hand on his arm again before leading her along the hall to the stairs. She was grateful that he said nothing as they walked to their appointed position behind Prince Zialni, just inside the front gates of the castle.

The distant cheers of the townspeople drifted to Alecia as the king made his way through the town. Red and gold silk bunting lined the path to the front entrance and the gravel had been swept clean. The servants were all in position in the red, white and gold uniform of House Zialni. Standing opposite her across the drive was Ramón. He wore a red and gold velvet tunic over spotless white breeches. His white gloves carried gold embroidery that matched the scabbard of his sword. His sharp blue eyes regarded her with frank admiration.

Alecia smiled at him. She missed Ramón's company and easy manner.

Vard cleared his throat. "A good-looking man, the squire," he said. "Don't let your father see you making calf eyes at him, though. He's not for you, I think."

Alecia turned to Vard. "Oh, and you would know to whom I am promised, would you? If that's the case, please tell me." Alecia bit her lip. She had not meant that last to pop out. She didn't want him to know that she had so little control of her life.

His gaze narrowed. "I didn't say I knew your father's mind, Princess, but I know enough to see that your father would never accept Zorba as your husband. It's a pity, as I think Zorba could make you happy, or happier than you..." He trailed off.

What had he been about to say? Happier than she deserved to be? Did he think so little of her? Sudden tears sprang up and she looked away. "I will not be content until my people are." She turned back to Vard and found him studying her, his gaze narrowed.

"That's rich coming from you," he said, quietly. "Your father is responsible for the suffering in Brightcastle."

"My father is not responsible," Alecia said, drawing closer to Vard so she could speak without being heard. "It's that unspeakable advisor who turns his heart against all that is right and good. You don't know him as I do."

"Your sight is colored by your love for your father, Princess. Lord Finus isn't to blame, at least not entirely."

"You have been in Brightcastle all of five minutes," she said coldly. "What can you know of anything?"

Vard's mouth snapped shut and Alecia turned her attention to the assembled servants.

Ramón's admiring look had become a scowl. A fanfare of trumpets blared and the King's party came into view. Rows of red-uniformed soldiers rode on white horses ahead of a polished redwood coach, with a golden Zialni crest on the carriage door. Behind followed three more coaches with different crests, that identified the passengers as minor royalty. Beyond that rode the servants on assorted horses, from ponies and palfreys to fierce-eyed stallions. Last of all came another group of soldiers on their prancing white mounts. Alecia suppressed an impulse to stand on tiptoe like a street urchin, instead wrapping herself in calm as she waited for her first glimpse of the King.

As the procession reached the castle gates, the double lines of soldiers peeled off to each side, allowing the King's carriage to enter the gravel drive. The carriage drew to a halt level with Prince Zialni, and a middle-aged man with the unmistakeable Zialni nose leaped out to engulf his brother in a bear hug. Alecia smiled at the sight even as she thanked the Goddess that she had escaped the curse of the large, hooked proboscis. Uncle Beniel was taller and thicker than her father, with none of Jiseve's grace, but his looks were still striking enough to turn heads. Despite becoming King, Beniel had lost none of his enthusiasm and zest for life.

"Alecia!" The king wrapped his arms around her and Alecia gasped as the silver braid on his dark military uniform scraped her cheek. "You are as beautiful as ever. So much like your mother." He sighed. "She was a marvel." He lowered his voice. "Jiseve has not been the same man since he lost Iona. She always was able to balance his darker moods."

Alecia frowned and glanced at her father, who wore his trademark scowl. He must have heard the King's words. Alecia hurried to introduce Vard.

"Captain," Beniel said as Vard rose from a bow. "See that you protect our niece. She is an important link in securing the Zialni claim to the throne of Thorius."

Vard's eyes swept over her briefly. "The safety of the princess is paramount, Your Majesty."

A dark-haired woman with tilted green eyes, wearing an emerald gown with silver thread over the bodice, appeared beside the King. She placed her hand on his arm. "Do you not think these discussions would be best conducted away from the ears of the servants, my dear?"

"Of course, my love. Here, greet our niece." Beniel drew Alecia forward. Queen Adriana's eyes were fixed on the captain and several moments passed before her aunt met her gaze.

"Alecia, dear," she said, "it is so very delicious to see you again." Alecia dropped into a low curtsy and was drawn to her feet by her aunt. Adriana's eyes were again on Vard. "Who is your escort?"

Vard stepped forward. "Captain Vard Anton, Your Majesty." He grasped queen's gloved hand and bowed. "If I can be of service to you in any way during your stay here, you've only to ask."

The queen seemed lost for words. Was there a woman alive that he could not entrance with his animal attraction?

Finally, Adriana recovered her poise. "Thank you, Captain. Perhaps I will save you a dance this evening."

Vard bowed again and stepped back as the regal couple moved on. There were other members of the royal party to be introduced but Alecia could not forget the exchange between her escort and the queen.

Eventually the king's entourage entered the foyer of the castle and Alecia found herself standing beside Ramón at the foot of the staircase.

"Hello, Princess. I've not seen you in several days." He made it sound as if she had been avoiding him.

"I have been unwell," Alecia said.

"Oh? Millie said nothing of your illness."

"I don't tell my maid every sniffle I suffer." She sounded defensive even to her ears.

"You *have* been avoiding me!"

"Don't flatter yourself," Alecia said. "Why would I avoid you anyway?"

"Because you have another on your mind." His eyes swept to Vard, where he stood chatting to Queen Adriana. "He's not the one for you, Alecia."

"Captain Anton is nothing to me but my guard."

"I've seen the way you stare at him. How your eyes follow him. He has the same effect on all the women he encounters, even the queen. I don't understand how he does it. He isn't that handsome."

"Ramón, you are prattling."

His eyes grew stormy. "Watch yourself with that man. I don't trust him and neither should you."

Alecia sighed. "I'll watch him. Now, will you dance with me tonight?"

Ramón frowned at the change of subject, however, as Alecia had suspected, the topic was too enticing to ignore. "Of course I will dance with you."

"Don't you have duties to attend to, Zorba?" Vard's deep tones had Alecia instantly distracted.

"Remember what I said, Princess," Ramón said. "Captain." He stalked away toward the kitchens, no doubt to supervise the preparation of the meal that was being laid in the formal dining room.

"I can't leave you for a moment, and that puppy scurries over," Vard said.

Alecia frowned. "He's hardly a puppy. He is the same age as I." She watched his jaw tighten. "Why do you dislike Ramón?"

"I have no feelings for the squire one way or another, but surely you can see that you and he can never enjoy your father's support?"

"He's a friend. Why can *you* not see that?"

"Princess, for all your twenty-four years, you've precious little knowledge of men. Squire Ramón isn't the tame friend you imagine."

"You're wrong." She was sick of the subject. "Can we talk of something else?"

He raised an eyebrow. "What topic had you in mind?"

"Yourself; the intriguing Captain Anton who has women falling at his feet and men desperate to best him with the sword."

He looked across the foyer and frowned. "Ask away."

"Where did you learn the longbow?"

Alecia's stomach tightened as the color drained from Vard's face. "Father taught me."

"Where is your father now?"

Vard seemed to have drifted away, his thoughts in another place. "I don't know. I was a lad when last I saw him. He could be dead for all I know."

Alecia suddenly had a premonition. "You'll find him one day. You must not stop searching."

His piercing gaze made her blink. "I've long given up hope of finding Papa. My purpose is to serve others. You do me no favours pretending prophecy."

Alecia dropped her eyes. *Goddess!* She hated it when those impressions hit her! They were like the dreams she had, and they were always true. Why was she cursed with them? Most people were like Vard and didn't want to know. "I'm sorry, Captain. I didn't mean to upset you." She searched for a safer topic. "You talk of service with almost religious zeal. It's unusual in a soldier."

He nearly smiled. "You're perceptive; that's nearer the truth than most come."

"There you go," Alecia said, "speaking in riddles again." *He would make a good poker player, this inscrutable man.* "What of your family, your mother, siblings…wife?"

Vard's poker face slipped and utter bleakness swept the light from his eyes. "I had a cousin who was like a brother. Frel and I did everything together." Alecia was reminded of the night in his room, and the pain in his voice brought sudden tears to her eyes.

"I must leave you for a time, Princess," he said, guiding her over to the doorway of the luncheon room and avoiding her gaze. "Your father has asked that you dine with the king and queen and then go to your chambers to prepare for the ball. I'll collect you at six this evening." He gave an abbreviated bow and strode through the doors of the dining room, every female eye following his departure.

At luncheon, Alecia picked at her food, distracted by Vard's reaction to her questions and her premonition. Tragedy lurked behind this mysterious cousin Frel, who was no longer in Vard's life. She itched to know the story, ached to make some of his pain go away. Perhaps he would allow her close enough to discover his secrets in time. It would mean risking her other self but she could no more ignore her enigmatic protector than banish the premonition that had struck her today. She was certain Vard was a part of her future – was that true intuition or just desire? Her father might plan her betrothal but how could she accept that fate now that she knew what she would be giving up?

At the end of the meal, the king himself escorted Alecia to her chambers.

"It is wonderful to see you again, niece. Adriana and I wish you could visit more often."

"It's a desire I've known as well, Uncle. Perhaps soon I'll visit you at Wildecoast."

"I would love nothing better, however I fear your father has plans that will make a visit impossible."

"You talk of my betrothal and marriage," Alecia said.

"That would not be a hurdle, Alecia, but your father plans for an heir as soon as possible. If you are with child, you must stay in Brightcastle. We cannot risk the heir to the kingdom."

"How can you talk like this when Aunt Adriana struggles so hard to give you a child? It must hurt her to know you plan for your succession with your great-nephew."

"The queen is a practical woman, Alecia, and knows we must secure the throne for our family. She herself has suggested I put her aside or take a mistress who can produce an heir. I would not do that to her. Surely you see that to bring a great-nephew to the throne is a lesser evil than that?"

She grasped Beniel's hands. "I'm not ready to bear a child, Uncle."

King Beniel's face grew stern. "You must do what is best for the kingdom, Alecia. Do not avoid your responsibilities. I will see you this evening."

He swept down the hallway. Alecia entered her apartment and drifted across to the painting of her mother that hung above her bed. The portrait depicted a sombre woman with straight blonde hair and pale blue eyes. Alecia's attention was caught by the determined set to her mother's mouth that she imagined she shared. Loneliness, which she usually managed to ignore, swamped her and she threw herself face down on her bed. She truly was on her own. Uncle Beniel would not be an ally. No one would stand in the way of her father's plans for her; she would be sacrificed for the Zialni name.

CHAPTER 11

THE sunlight cast long golden patches on the slate floor beneath her windows when Alecia finally awoke. Her head ached from the tears she had shed, but tonight she would conduct herself as she knew her mother would have – with dignity and strength. Her father and uncle wouldn't see the pain they caused with their ultimatums and arrangements. Vard wouldn't intimidate her with his warnings. She was a princess of the people.

However, when Alecia saw her face she doubted she could survive even the next few minutes, let alone the gruelling night ahead. Dark smudges lay beneath her eyes and tears had left tracks down her cheeks. Her eyes belonged to a frightened girl, not a courageous young woman. *All will be well if I just keep moving.*

She scrubbed her face in cold water and used some of Hetty's concealing lotion to fix the darkness beneath her eyes. By the time Millie arrived, Alecia had lined her eyes with kohl and applied rouge and lip balm. She was able to smile at the woman in the mirror now.

"You look beautiful, Princess," the maid said. "The captain won't be able to take his eyes off you." Millie teased the strands of Alecia's hair into an elaborate twist. "I just saw him, Highness, striding through the castle, his eyes everywhere."

"I dare say he is trying to ensure the safety of all who attend the ball tonight." Alecia couldn't see how Millie did such an expert job with her hair while rabbiting on about Vard.

"He could do that in his sleep, Princess." Millie finished the creation and sprayed Alecia's hair with another concoction of Hetty's that was designed to hold the style. "There's something else on that man's mind, just as His Highness is planning some excitement for this evening. You mark my words."

Alecia pushed Millie's words from her thoughts; getting through the evening with Vard as escort was enough to contemplate.

Millie laid the gold Zialni tiara in Alecia's hair. "You're a picture, Princess. Now for the dress." She helped Alecia out of her crushed blue gown and into the cream satin, making light work of the pearl buttons that created a stunning feature at the back. The round neckline of this gown was more modest than the blue Alecia had worn earlier, but still left her shoulders bare. Sparkling amethyst gems at her throat and ears completed the ensemble.

Alecia slid her feet into the cream satin slippers and crossed to the full-length mirror. She could hardly believe the transformation. Her lilac eyes shone without a trace of the weariness and fear that had been there before.

A quiet knock sounded at her door and Millie scurried out to answer it. Alecia followed and stood in the doorway to her bedroom. The maid swept such a deep curtsy that Alecia expected her father or the king to be standing without; instead Vard stepped over the threshold. He came to an abrupt halt as he saw Alecia.

His eyes swept from the toes of her slippers to the tiara in her hair and Alecia was certain he had not missed a single detail. She would have blushed only she could not take her eyes from him.

There was something different about him this evening, his presence heightened far beyond even his usual magnetism. Alecia could not see what had caused it. He looked the perfect picture of an army captain: fit, hard and disciplined. The familiar gilt flecks in his eyes glowed, their intensity framed by his dark curls, tanned skin and sensuous mouth; a mouth that curved into a mocking smile. Millie was right. Something absorbed his attention, focused his desire. Alecia did blush at *that* thought.

"Go and offer the queen your help, Millie," Alecia said. "I no longer require your presence."

"Yes, Princess." Millie curtsied and left, the door banging shut behind her.

Vard cleared his throat. "You're beautiful, Princess."

Her insides grew warm under his gaze but she remembered her pledge to make her mother proud. *He's just a man.* Her stomach lurched at the thought but she squashed the panic she felt at being alone with him and smiled. "Thank you. You look dashing tonight." The words sounded awkward.

He did not smile again, just looked at her, a tiny frown on his brow. Too late, she remembered to look away. Keeping her secret from Vard had seemed less important since the kiss.

She walked across to her dresser to retrieve the drawstring bag that contained her powders and blusher and then sprayed her neck with liberal quantities of the floral perfume she kept for special occasions. When Alecia turned back to Vard, he was right behind her, his body tensed as though ready to fight...or run, his eyes burning with potency.

"Are you well, Captain?" Excitement and fear charged her body. Perhaps it was contagious.

He blinked and seemed to relax a little. "I'm well," he said, "but I can see you're nervous. I'll keep you safe; you must do your best to enjoy the evening." He smiled suddenly, one of the first real smiles Alecia had seen on him. "I certainly look forward to the company of a beautiful woman tonight."

Alecia peered up at him. His smile had ignited a warm glow low in her belly and she was drawn to him as if she had no free will. Unable to look away, she stepped closer and laid her hands on his chest. He tensed, his gaze falling to her mouth and then darting around her face before coming to rest on her eyes once again. His throat spasmed as if he warred with some emotion.

She braced herself for his rejection but kept her eyes on his, willing him to accept what she offered. Slowly his arms came around her waist and crushed her against his hard maleness. Her heart beat wildly, or was it his? They stood like that for long moments, welded in the embrace, Alecia drinking in his heady scent, her body alive to his touch, yearning for the thrill of his skin against hers. She brought her hands up to place some distance between them, but Vard's arm moved up her back to cup the base of her skull. He tilted her head until their eyes met once more. His irises revealed the depth of his arousal: mere bands of gold around swollen pupils. Alecia's heart leaped as she watched his lips descend to hers.

His mouth was hard, demanding, his lips possessing hers from the first touch. As she responded, arching her body against his, his tongue forced its way into her mouth and she moaned at the intimate exploration. Alecia pulled his face hard against hers, her fingers trapped in his hair, her tongue probing with a life of its own. Now it was Vard's turn to groan and his hands roved over her back and buttocks, kneading the soft tissue there and pulling her against the bulge in his breeches. Her body betrayed her desire, pushing closer, wanting him inside her.

Vard walked backwards with her, their mouths fused as one. Alecia hardly knew what she did. Her body moved of its own accord, desperate to sate the explosive need that had built low in her abdomen. She fell onto him as he lay back on her bed. He pulled her leg across his hip and raised her skirt in one practised motion. The warmth of his fingers crept up the back of her knee. It only served to heat her blood further. She didn't object as Vard reached up inside the long leg of her pantaloons and then rolled her onto her back. His weight trapped her as he raised himself to look down on her.

"Is this what you want for your first time, Alecia?" A muscle tensed along his jaw as he waited for her reply.

She swallowed and tried to form the words that would reassure him, but the tumult of emotions tied her tongue. She nodded, her eyes unable to leave his face for fear that if she broke the contact, he would walk away from her.

Alecia poured all the hunger inside her into her gaze and seized the hair at the nape of his neck, determined to finish what she had started. He groaned and lowered his lips to hers once more, this time more sensually, bringing her to the peak of longing. Her hips strained against his and she cursed the fabric that separated their skins, anticipating the firestorm that would consume them when all barriers were stripped away.

The inhibitions she had felt with their first kiss were gone. Alecia moaned as Vard pulled the shoulders of her gown down her arms to expose the swell of her breasts. His lips caressed the exposed skin while her hands raked his shirt below his tunic. Vard paused long enough to shrug out of his tunic, and strip the shirt from his body, before lowering his head to her neck once more.

"I want you," Alecia said, her voice tense with need. "Take me now… please."

He rolled onto his side and pulled her around to face him, his eyes almost completely black. She ran her fingers through the hair at the top of his chest and let them slide down his abdomen. His skin felt hot enough to scorch, but it was nothing beside the heat in her core. She knelt on the coverlet, undid the pearl buttons she could reach and then sat back on her heels.

Slowly, Vard crouched before her and pulled the creamy material down her arms. His teeth grasped the satin over her breasts and tugged until her snowy mounds were freed, the nipples standing pink and erect. He rolled her onto her back and she gasped as his lips and tongue caressed first one nipple and then the other. She was lost in a torrent of mad desire. Her only thought was to push this man to the brink and then fall over it with him.

As Vard's hands pushed her skirts up, his mouth continued to ravish her breasts. Her body moved of its own volition, hips straining upwards in open invitation. He teased her pantaloons off and she moaned in anticipation, gasping as his fingers found the slick wetness between her thighs. There was only one thing she wanted now and it must be soon or she would explode. Alecia groaned and fumbled at the waist of his breeches. Fulfilment was so close she could taste it. The very fibres of her being hummed in tune with Vard's. His hard manhood pushed against her; she knew it would fill her, satiate her.

A gong sounded. She barely heard it. It was nothing; an annoyance, a distraction.

Vard froze, poised over her. "What are we doing?" he said, his voice barely recognisable. He pried her fingers from his breeches, pulled her skirt down to hide her desire and swung his body from the bed. "Cover yourself."

Cold shock struck Alecia. How could he pull away? This was all she wanted. She stood, kicked her pantaloons from her ankles and faced him, her breasts still exposed above the neck of her gown.

His eyes fell to her chest and he groaned. "I can't have you." He reached for her but instead of caressing her flesh, he tugged at her dress to cover her nudity. His fingers trailed over the satin of her bodice as they dropped to his sides.

Shudders ripped through her body at his touch. The pressure in her loins was almost a physical pain. She reached for him again. That was where all this had started. She buried her face in the hair of his chest, breathing in his scent and letting her fingers trickle through the hair that ran down to the waist of his breeches.

Vard pushed her away and reached for his shirt. "That's the gong to announce the beginning of festivities. We'll be missed."

"If that's all you're worried about," Alecia said. "I can call Millie and say I'm unwell."

He paused in buttoning his shirt and she thought she had won. "Fix your hair and face, Princess. I'll wait outside."

"No!" Alecia took two steps and flung herself into his arms, arching her body against his. His rock-hard arousal assailed her through the layers of her skirts. His pupils contracted and dilated as the war raged within him. He could not refuse her now!

Vard grasped her wrists and pushed her away. "Your body invites me, tempts me, but we mustn't let our desires rule. A woman like you, a princess, should save herself for her husband."

He tried to walk past her and Alecia wrapped her arm around his waist, her face so close to his that she breathed his ragged exhalation. The war still thundered within him.

"A moment ago, you had forgotten what I am," she said, "Take me now, *please*." Giddy exultation surged through her as he bent his mouth to hers again, but his lips were like granite as he ravished her, leaving Alecia in shock at his brutality.

"It's been fun, Princess," he said, his mocking smile belittling everything they had just shared. "I'll wait outside." Vard left and the door closed with a sharp click.

CHAPTER 12

ALECIA stood, too dazed to move. The fire of her desire still burned but there was a cold lump in the pit of her stomach. She had thrown herself at him, begged him to ravish her and he had rejected her. *Again.* Thank the Goddess that she had not coupled with him. What was she thinking? *I begged him!* And truth be known, she would still allow it should he return. How could she hide the torrent of her emotions from the eyes of the partygoers?

The mirror showed her dress in disarray, bodice sagging and skirts rumpled. She straightened the bodice and laboured over the buttons at her back. Her face heated as she spied her pantaloons on the floor by the bed. She pulled them on and smoothed her skirt, then returned to the mirror.

Her hair was a bit squashed at the back but she ran her fingers through the jumbled tresses and managed to restore the style to respectability. Then she repainted her face with a shaking hand. The results were acceptable, but she knew she wouldn't fool Millie if the maid were to see her. She retrieved her purse, slipped on her satin shoes and opened her chamber door.

Vard waited for her, resplendent in his dark uniform. His features were composed as he held out his arm for her hand. There was no recognition in his gaze of what they had shared. Her body began to tremble as she realized how close she had come to losing herself to this man. She determined to put the experience out of her mind. They made their way down the hall to the top of the stairs, where Ramón waited.

"Good evening, Princess," Ramon said, bowing. "Captain."

Alecia's throat clogged. She coughed and found her voice. "Good evening." She smiled, striving to regain her composure, to appear the woman she had been before Vard's rejection. "Do you have no one on your arm tonight?"

"The prince has not requested my services, and so I am free to dance with whomever I please. I hope you'll save me one." His blond locks were tied back in a band and he wore a cream silk coat over black breeches.

"Of course." Her words were for Ramón but every particle of her being was in tune with her escort. And she sensed his growing impatience.

"Excuse us, Zorba." Vard stepped off with Alecia down the stairs.

"Oh Goddess!" she muttered. In seconds she would have to face the curious stares of her father's guests when all she desired was to curl up and forget the rest of the world existed. At the base of the staircase she stopped.

Vard turned to her, clearly puzzled by the abrupt halt. "What's amiss?" His gaze met hers and the rest of the world fell away.

"I can't face those people tonight," she said. "Take me somewhere where I can be alone."

A muscle in his jaw tightened. "That wouldn't be wise on many accounts. This event won't be as odious as you imagine. I'll stay by your side."

"Will you? You didn't give that impression just a few minutes ago in my room." She clamped her mouth shut to stem the flow of words that threatened to spill. "We can't leave things between us as they are."

Vard opened his mouth to reply but at that moment, the master of ceremonies spied them. He announced their names and Alecia suppressed a shudder as all eyes turned to them.

The ballroom was almost full. The guild masters were in attendance with their wives, as were several of the minor country lords. Others she didn't recognize must be members of the King's retinue. His Majesty and the queen had not arrived. Ramón was announced, pounced upon by a gaggle of young women and drawn away to the buffet table.

"Can I fetch you a drink, Princess?" Vard gazed down at her. If he was upset by what had passed between them in her chambers, he didn't show it. *It's better this way.* She would bury her feelings for Vard deep, where they would not trouble her. Even as she made the decision, her body betrayed her, nerve endings tuned to his presence. She could have found him in a crowded room with her eyes closed.

"Wine would be nice."

As Alecia waited for her drink, King Beniel and Queen Adriana stepped through the doorway to thunderous applause. Her aunt was elegant in a crimson gown that hugged her figure to the thigh and then fell in full lace ruffles to hide her feet. The strapless silk dress was complemented by full-length red silk gloves. A ruby choker encased Adriana's neck and extended over her shoulders and chest, much like chain mail. As Alecia moved forward to greet the royal couple she saw that the queen's choker was indeed made from silver rings, interlinked, with rubies set about the entire piece.

She curtsied before the royal couple and King Beniel drew her into his embrace.

"Alecia, my dear, you are ravishing this evening. How am I to claim you for a dance? I will have to fight off the young men…and the not so young."

Alecia laughed. "Nonsense, Uncle, you're still the most handsome man here. Besides Father, of course." She smiled at the queen. "That's a striking necklace, Aunt."

Queen Adriana kissed her niece on both cheeks. "It is just something my master jeweller fashioned for me," she said. "He knows how I adore watching the knights on the tourney field and thought it would amuse me to wear chain mail. Quaint, is it not?"

Alecia murmured agreement but the queen's attention shifted. The monarch suddenly reminded Alecia of a hunting lioness.

"Your wine, Princess," Vard said.

Alecia took the embossed silver goblet from Vard. He swept the king and queen a low bow then rose and took Adriana's offered hand. "You look exquisite, Your Majesty."

"You are kind, Captain."

The orchestra chose that moment to play a lively tune that heralded the beginning of the dance music for the evening. Queen Adriana stepped closer to Vard and spoke into his ear. Alecia's nails dug into her palm as her escort swept the queen away, the first of many couples who took to the dance floor. Ramón had a buxom blonde in his arms and Prince Zialni danced with the wife of the master goldsmith. Alecia glared at Vard and her aunt, stupid tears threatening. *How dare he leave me in the corner?*

"May I have this dance, niece?" The King's strong arms swept her among the other dancers. The style of dance was such that partners were changed on a regular basis, and she soon found herself with Vard. He pulled her close against him and she fought the urge to melt into his arms, her heart pounding so hard she couldn't concentrate on the steps. Where had a soldier learned to dance with such flair?

"Please accept my apologies," he murmured against her hair. "The queen is difficult to refuse." His strong arms guided her expertly around the floor and into Ramón's at the next change.

"That man dances well for a soldier," Ramón said. "Do you wonder how?"

"It had not occurred to me to wonder," she said, still thinking of Vard's apology. Apparently she, Alecia, was all too easy to reject.

"What's wrong, Princess? What has he done to you now?"

"Why do you think he has done anything?"

"He has hurt you!"

"Keep your voice down! This is none of your business." She flew from his arms into the sweaty paws of another guild master and then into those of Lord Finus.

"Your beauty dazzles me tonight, Princess Alecia." The lord's eyes gleamed, his dark gaze lingering on her bosom. "Did you have the dress made for this occasion?"

Alecia clenched her teeth to hold back her anger. "No, Lord Finus. I wore this gown to my debut at the King's palace. I wouldn't expect you to know. You weren't with us then, were you?"

Lord Finus frowned and Alecia's heart lightened as her subtle barb hit home. He didn't like to be reminded that his influence with the prince, though strong, had yet to stand the test of time. Her father was the next man to take her in his arms.

"Are you enjoying the dance so far, Daughter?" Prince Zialni said.

"It is a fine gathering, Father. Uncle Beniel is delighted."

"I did not plan this celebration for Beniel. There is a rather more special reason for the ball tonight." He focused on her properly. "You look lovely. I am proud to call you daughter." The song finished and he squeezed her hand. "We will talk again later. Until then, enjoy yourself."

Prince Zialni left the dance floor and was immediately surrounded by guild masters and their wives. Several had goblets of wine, which they offered to her father. He declined all and had his personal hand-servant refill his wine glass. No doubt he feared drugs or poison.

Alecia retrieved her goblet of wine from the table where she had left it and allowed her eyes to wander over the crowd. Vard escorted Adriana back to Beniel's side and his eyes met hers across the room. She raised the goblet to her mouth and he shook his head and began to move toward her. Alecia suppressed the sudden urge to drink the wine anyway.

When he reached her he took the goblet, lifted it to his nose and inhaled deeply. "The wine is safe, Princess, but don't drink from any vessel this night that hasn't come from my hands or that of the prince's servant." He handed the wine back to her and she downed it in one go.

"What *are* you?" Alecia asked, mentally listing all the reasons that Vard was like no other man.

He stiffened. "Suffice to say that I can detect poison in food and wine." He studied her, appearing to take in every aspect of her face.

"I think we both know I wasn't speaking of the wine." Heat rose in her bosom and all of a sudden her head was fuzzy, the rest of the room falling away until she and Vard stood in their own cocoon. He grasped her by the elbow, the intensity of his gaze making the breath catch in her throat. Had he changed his mind?

"Come with me, Princess," he said. "I'll fetch you some food to have with your wine."

Suddenly she could breathe again. How could she make such a fool of herself over a man? "I'll wait here," she said. Perhaps some distance would allow her to banish her silly fancies.

Vard frowned but acquiesced to her wishes and slipped into the crowd that lay between him and the food-laden tables.

She chewed her bottom lip as she watched him go.

Ramón appeared at her side. He pulled her around to face him and held both her hands, his baby-blue eyes serious. "Now what did he do to you?"

Alecia's eyebrows arched. "Who?"

"You know of whom I speak," he said.

"Vard has gone to get me some food."

"Since when have you called him Vard?"

Alecia couldn't help flinching. *Trust me to open my big mouth.* "He has asked me to call him Vard when we are alone."

Ramón studied her. "Something has occurred between you and Anton," he said. "You're treating him differently."

Alecia thought, not for the first time, that Ramón was very perceptive. "You imagine things. We've just had a disagreement." She pulled her hands from his. "I need some air." She pushed her way through the crowd and out to the terrace.

It was warm so she stepped off the pavers and onto the grass, heading for the first row of trees. A few moments of fresh air should restore her composure and allow her fuzzy mind to clear. Then she could return to the ball. Unfortunately, Ramón followed and seated himself beside her on the stone bench under an oak tree.

"I want to be alone." She relaxed back into the seat and closed her eyes.

"It's not safe for you to be out here alone, Princess…Alecia…"

"Nonsense, Father has increased the patrols both inside and outside the castle walls. I'm perfectly safe." Her eyes remained closed, her thoughts on Vard and the moments they had shared.

"I don't like to see you like this." There was real concern in his voice.

She opened her eyes. It was too dark to see the expression on the his face.

"Ever since Anton came," he said, "you've been distant from me. I miss you. I want to help you."

Alecia reached out and took his hand. "Just be my friend."

"I can't be your friend if I can't even see you." He pulled Alecia around so that she faced him, and his hands remained on her arms. "I've realized one thing." His hands tightened until they hurt. "I love you, Alecia."

Ramón's mouth drifted closer. Would his kiss feel different to Vard's? One kiss couldn't hurt. She let his mouth cover hers. Ramón's lips were gentle and his arms crept around her, pulling her close. The faint scent of lemon and cloves clung to his skin. She closed her eyes, snaking her arms under his and up his back.

Ramón's arms tightened and his mouth became more demanding, his tongue pushing past her lips. Alecia arched against him but her mind stayed remote as if viewing the seduction from afar. His hand slid down her back and along her thigh. Alecia knew what they did was wrong. She tried to pull away but his arm held her so tightly she could barely breathe. The first stirrings of panic fluttered in her stomach as his other hand pulled her skirts slowly up her leg. *No!* She thumped his chest with both hands but was held too close for her efforts to have any impact. Finally, she dragged her mouth from his.

"Let me go," she gasped, panting.

Ramón's mouth lowered to her throat. The hand that had been pulling up her skirts moved to her left breast and Alecia squirmed away.

"Ramón," she said, her voice breathy, "I don't want this." She pulled free and stood up, frantically smoothing her dress for the second time that evening. He came after her, his hands grasping her shoulders and pulling her against him. Alecia struggled against him, aware of his strength and his maleness as she never had been before. *Vard was right! Ramón is not some tame puppy I can lead around on a string!*

"You could love me, Alecia. I know you could. Come with me to my room. Let me show you how good we could be together."

"She's not going anywhere with you, Zorba," a deep voice said.

Alecia bounded back as Ramón's hands fell from her shoulders.

Vard stepped from the shadows behind the oak. His eyes, aglow in the dim light from the terrace, sent shivers up Alecia's spine.

Ramón drew himself to his full height, almost that of Vard's. "I've watched you, Anton. You seek to come between Alecia and myself for your own reasons. You're not concerned for her safety."

"If her safety was your priority, you wouldn't allow her to remain in this garden," Vard said. "I've just proven that anything could lurk in the shadows. Return to the party. There's a string of beauties eager to dance with you. Try your luck with them."

Alecia gasped at the crude remark and Ramón tensed, his fists bunched and his jaw jutting toward Vard. The two eyed each other off and just when Alecia thought Ramón would attack, he spun and stalked back toward the ballroom. She sighed with relief, surprised to see that Ramón moved with the athletic grace of a swordsman. When had that happened?

"I told you he was dangerous," Vard said.

"He would never hurt me."

"He loves you and would do anything to have you. Worse, he lies to himself, and that is what makes him dangerous. He tells himself that you return his feelings, that it's only a matter of time before you come to your senses. Don't place yourself in this position again."

"You're a fine one to talk, Captain. Is my honor safe with you?"

Vard swallowed, his mouth thinning. "It seems so. I remember a certain young woman begging me to take her earlier this evening. It's no thanks to you that I didn't."

"A moment of weakness. Believe me, I won't make the same mistake again."

"You'll make that mistake over and over. You're a slave to your desires. Once awakened, they crave fulfilment, but the squire is not the man to give you what you need."

Alecia laughed out loud. So she was a slave to her desires, was she? She stepped close to Vard and looked up into eyes that burned like the sun. "Who is the man to give me fulfilment? You awakened my desire. Will you now sate it?"

If she could have had those words back, Alecia would have. Vard's irises swelled, huge and glowing, his jaw clenched and his hands balled into fists. He groaned, the sound like that of a tortured animal, and his right hand moved upwards. She stepped backwards, but Vard didn't reach for her. He clutched the stone at his throat and closed his eyes. As she watched, the anger left his face and when he opened his eyes, they appeared normal. "Your father has an announcement to make. Come and dance with me before you are missed."

He escorted her back to the party, his hand rock-solid under her left elbow, and swept her onto the dance floor for a waltz. His thighs moved beside hers, arms strong and sure on her body. She fought for control for a few minutes and then surrendered. He was an expert dancer, so skilled that she closed her eyes and lost herself in the music and the movement of their bodies. Yes, Vard had been the man who had awakened her desire, and she could never have enough of him, but she would be naïve to believe he felt the same.

Too soon, the waltz ended and Vard handed her to the King. She barely noticed the next few dances, so lost was she in the memories of the dance shared with her protector. Her heart leaped as Vard reclaimed her from the master goldsmith for a stately ronde that was in vogue at court, but Alecia longed for the intimacy of the waltz.

The trumpet player blew a fanfare and all eyes turned to the small stage at the front of the room. Alecia raised her eyebrows at Vard and he shook his head. He didn't seem to know the subject of the announcement either.

Prince Zialni took the stage, magnificent in his black velvet trousers and jacket. The silver edging of his cloak flared as he flung out his arms.

"My good people," he said. "I would like to thank my brother, King Beniel, and his lovely queen, Adriana, for attending this humble gathering. Thanks also to the esteemed members of the King's court and to my other distinguished guests. I have a joyous announcement to make. One I have long waited for. It concerns my beautiful daughter, Alecia." He turned to Vard. "Captain Anton, would you escort the princess to the stage?"

Vard guided Alecia through the crowd to her father's side, bowed and departed. Alecia felt his absence keenly. The stares of the guests bored into her and she was drunk from the wine and the echo of Vard's strong arms around her.

The prince cleared his throat. "It is my pleasure to announce the betrothal of my daughter, the Princess Alecia Allandra Dosodra Zialni, to a man who has become a crucial link in my tenure here. He is my future son-in-law, Lord Giornan Finus."

CHAPTER 13

VARD quashed his rage and inched closer to where Alecia stood on the stage. The princess swayed, red spots flaring in pale cheeks, as Finus made his way to her side. The prospective bridegroom couldn't take his eyes from his prize. Vard saw only greed in his gaze. Perhaps he'd been too harsh on Alecia. She was as much the victim as anyone, a pawn in Prince Zialni's plan to secure his hold on the Kingdom of Thorius. It seemed others approved of the match, if King Beniel's grin was any indication. A growl bubbled up within him. Alecia wouldn't accept this.

The princess needed time to recover from her shock, and not under the stares of the guests. Lord Finus kissed her on both cheeks and then led her down the stairs to the dance floor. The music signalled a stately court promenade, not a waltz, and for that Vard was glad. His hackles rose at the thought of Alicia's scent melded with that of her betrothed.

Vard glanced around the ball room in an attempt to distract himself, to regain his composure, but all eyes were on the couple in the centre of the floor. In seconds, he found Alecia again, dancing like a life-sized doll, stiff and unyielding. The image of her naked in Finus's arms flashed through his mind, and his rage became a living thing, boiling up through his core. He grasped the talisman, battling the animal that beat at him from within.

Distance was what he needed; distance from his emotions, from his inner turmoil and from this town, where life had become so complicated. A vice tightened in his chest, the control of the stone replaced by the panic of a trapped beast. Lord Finus led Alecia to the edge of the dance floor and left her alone. The princess bolted into the garden and Vard followed.

The freedom of the garden helped to calm the restless creature within, and Vard poured all of his rage into the stone. Eventually his wolf focus shifted to man and it was safe to approach.

Alecia sat on the stone bench under the oak, dry-eyed, staring at her left hand, seeming unaware of him as he sat beside her.

"He will place a ring here." She clutched her left index finger. "I would rather die than be married to that man. I will breathe my last before I let him bed me." Finally she looked at Vard and he flinched at the hurt in her eyes.

He didn't touch her. "You've known the prince would arrange your marriage." His voice held a ragged note. It wouldn't take much to push him out of control. *I should go now.* "Come back inside, Princess."

Alecia shook her head. "I believed my father would act in my best interests, even while he chose my husband." She tugged at her ring finger as if she hoped to pull it from her hand. "He has shown he cares nothing for me – or at least cares less for me than for himself and the kingdom. Lord Finus has truly corrupted him."

"It's not just Finus. You must see that."

Her eyes wandered over his face. "I don't know what I see any more. Death would be better than this."

"There was a time when I felt the same," Vard said. "That I'd rather die than live. I felt that way for so long, I thought it would always be so."

He had Alecia's whole attention now. She looked at him as if she had never truly seen him before, as if he were her lifeline. "Tell me what you did to heal yourself."

Vard closed his eyes to block the desperation in her gaze. There was no hope for Alecia in his story. His cure was not for her. He opened his eyes. "I found someone who understood me, who could guide me. I lost him too soon. Still, he helped me from that black place."

Alecia reached out and snagged his upper arms. "Help me, Vard. Please. You can't stand by and let this happen."

"What would you have me do?" Vard crushed the angry words that wanted to leap from his mouth. He could kill the prince and it wouldn't change this. He could kill Lord Finus but who would take his place? He could carry Alecia from this kingdom but he was more dangerous to her than anyone he could think of. "There's nothing I can do, Princess, but I won't let you kill yourself."

Her hands tightened on his arms. "Then you are cruel beyond measure. Are you so pitiless that you would not look the other way while I took my life?"

Vard wrenched his arms free of Alecia's grasp and stood before her, his breath coming in ragged gulps. Why should her words hurt him?

Something smashed into him from behind and a searing pain hit the right side of his chest. He sagged onto Alecia and glanced down at the sharp tip of a crossbow bolt protruding from his shirt below his right breast. Alecia's eyes bulged as a dark stain spread across his shirt.

Agony almost made him black out but he lurched toward the transformation, animal terror dulling the spasms that racked his chest. He twisted and the pain doubled. He searched the night shadows even as his vision blurred and shifted. Just as a faint rustle alerted him to the intruder in the bush twenty paces away, another bolt took him in his left shoulder. As Vard fell to hands and knees he knew he left Alecia vulnerable. He scrambled desperately to force his body into the change that could save his life; one that would be less of a threat to Alecia – the wolf.

* * *

Alecia knelt beside Vard, her heart fluttering at the sight of the bolts protruding from his back and shoulder. Bloodstains spread from the metal lodged in his body. Her eyes met his golden ones and she shivered at the dull gleam in their depths.

"Run, Alecia!" Vard's words were little more than a strangled gasp. *How can he survive?*

Fear tightened her chest, forcing her to take quick panting breaths as she searched for the attacker. She must help Vard, draw the gaze of the shooter so that her captain would live. Already he slumped, his fingers curling, his knees drawn to his chest.

Alecia bent over him. "Vard, let me help you inside."

He looked up at her, eyes wild. "Leave me!" The words were barely comprehensible. "Save yourself." He growled and Alecia backed away as he fought his way to his hands and knees, his gaze locked with hers. Alecia blinked to clear her vision as his body swelled, encapsulated by a nimbus of white light. He was indistinct, his margins fuzzy. The hand that clutched the grass had broadened and now looked more like a paw. Her insides froze, the world shrinking to encompass only herself and Vard. Time slowed as the man before her swelled and shrank then swelled again. She couldn't be seeing what she thought she was. A groan that was more a growl escaped from her protector and Alecia snapped into the present. She backed away, prepared to flee, but unable to accept the vision before her.

In Vard's place was a huge brown bear. Its paws were the size of dinner plates and it must have weighed more than two horses. Alecia couldn't look away as the beast turned to her, saliva dripping from its canines. Golden eyes gleamed and its huge, wet nose twitched, taking her scent. She could not see the wounds made by the crossbow bolts. Plans of escape formulated themselves in her mind but she could never outrun this creature, especially dressed as she was.

The bear that must be Vard – she had to accept that – reared up onto its hind legs. She slapped her hands over her ears as it roared, teeth bared, drool spraying over her. Its foul breath caressed her face and still she couldn't scream. Someone would hear the creature and investigate, but by then it would be too late. The bear roared again and a twig snapped in the bushes behind the beast. It dropped to all fours and gave her a hungry look before whirling to face the noise. Then it swung its head back toward Alecia and she saw her death in its feral eyes. It reared up onto its back legs again and Alecia fell to her knees, resigned to her fate. She closed her eyes, too scared to witness its final lunge, but giant steps carried the beast away from her.

Relief swept over Alecia and she slumped to the grass, sobs shaking her shoulders. Bile rose in her throat and she emptied her stomach, retching until her insides ached. When she wiped her hand across her mouth, her fingers were ice-cold.

"Here she is," a dreaded oily voice said.

Her stomach cramped and she retched again. *Not him! Please, Goddess, I can't deal with him now.*

"Are you well, my dear?" Lord Finus said. "What has passed here?" He drew her to her feet and tried to place his arm around her shoulders.

"Let me go," she said, shrugging him away.

A crowd of partygoers had poured from the ballroom. Prince Zialni sent for his troops while King Beniel stood with his arms around his wife. Adriana slipped from the King's embrace and moved toward Alecia. Ramón glanced at Alecia and dashed into the dark garden. *Oh Goddess, keep him safe.* She had to find Vard before he harmed someone or was harmed. What was she saying? He already had mortal injuries. A thread inside her snapped and she started to tremble.

Finus twisted her to face him.

Alecia's blood grew colder. She couldn't think past the need to escape. "Don't touch me," she said, her words sluggish and lacking conviction. She tugged at her hands caught in his, trying to pull free, looking toward the forest where Vard had disappeared. "I must search for him." Alecia didn't care whom Finus thought she referred to. The dreaded hands tightened their grip until they hurt.

"I will not allow you to place yourself in further peril," Finus hissed. "Tell me what happened."

She glared at him. He wasn't her lord and master yet; she hoped he never would be.

"Answer Giornan's question, Alecia," Prince Zialni said, his voice commanding.

She turned to her father. "There was a man out here with a crossbow." Alecia paused, not certain how much to tell, not certain what she believed. "He shot the captain twice."

"Are you unharmed?"

Alecia couldn't absorb the question. Scrambled thoughts and pictures fluttered about her brain. Vard pierced by the crossbow bolts, the surprise in his eyes, slow blood spreading, the bear, fear, cold. "Yes."

"She is in shock, Your Highness," Lord Finus said. "Let me escort her to her chambers." He placed his arm around Alecia's waist but she pulled out of his grasp.

"I told you not to touch me." Alecia heard a gasp, perhaps from the queen, but she didn't care. Let them think what they would.

"Alecia does not know what she says," Finus said. Even through her frozen mind, she could tell he was furious. The slimy toad was angry that she didn't fall at his feet with instant love and obedience? She would make it her mission to show him the mistake he had made on agreeing to this betrothal. Her mouth cracked a grim smile. Better to focus on Finus than on the bear and Vard.

King Beniel cleared his throat. "Can I suggest that we return to the castle to discuss this? It is hardly helping the princess to stand here in the cold when she has had a fright."

"Quite so, Brother." Prince Zialni took Alecia's arm in his and she was glad of his support as he guided her back to the ballroom. He spoke quiet words to the musicians and they returned to their instruments. The tune they played soothed her raw nerves a little. The prince led her to a chair and made her sit. Someone pushed a goblet of mulled wine into her hands. The heat returned to her fingertips as she sipped the warm, sweet liquid.

Alecia was vaguely aware of the guests being dismissed and of her father's soldiers arriving with torches to begin the search for the intruder. The men gathered just inside the doors while the queen and her ladies-in-waiting clustered around Alecia.

"What a shock you have had, Niece," Adriana said, "and on your betrothal night, too. Do not think this is an ill omen for your nuptials. All will be well."

Alecia looked up at the queen. She was so beautiful and self-assured. Had Adriana's marriage been arranged for her? She *seemed* happy. "All will never be well again."

Queen Adriana laughed. "Oh, Alecia, you are so melodramatic. The soldiers will catch this foul trespasser and life will return to normal."

"That's not what I'm referring to." Alecia's voice was cold. "Can you have someone fetch my maid? I wish to return to my room."

The queen grasped the arm of a passing serving girl and spoke a few quiet words. The girl's face blanched at being addressed by the monarch, but she gathered her skirts and ran from the room.

Alecia watched her father, Lord Finus and King Beniel as they talked in low tones near the outer door. Finus fixed her with his cold eyes and then stalked over.

"Princess, I must ask you about the noise we heard."

Alecia held her tongue.

"Yes," Queen Adriana said. "I heard the roar of a bear. Tell us about it, my dear."

"There was a brown bear in the garden," Alecia said. "I don't know how it came to be there."

"A bear and a crossbow-wielding intruder," Finus said. "The garden was crowded this night. There is also the question of how the invader eluded the patrols."

Prince Zialni joined the group. "Patrols you were responsible for, Finus. The very same patrols that allowed an assassin close enough to shoot my daughter's protector."

"Is it not a little hasty to name the invader an assassin, Your Highness?" Finus smiled a sickly smile and Alecia's insides warmed a little at his discomfort.

"What else can this be but an assassination attempt? My daughter, your betrothed, might have been murdered this night and you stand here debating? You will find out what happened to the patrols and how this man came to penetrate the castle defenses."

"I assure you I will do so and bring this intruder to justice, Your Highness," Finus said, "but what of the bear?"

"The bear won't get far," Prince Zialni said. "In the morning, my men will track it and kill it. We cannot have rogue animals menacing the palace. The assassin may be a more difficult matter, unless he has left a trace of his passing. I'll question the soldiers on patrol myself. You said Captain Anton was wounded, Alecia. Where is he now? Why did he leave you alone in the garden?"

Alecia frowned and bit her lip. Considering Vard's wounds, she doubted he would ever return. Unbidden, his handsome face filled her thoughts; the memory of his embrace lent her comfort. But she would never again find solace in Vard's arms. If by chance he should survive, how could she face him after what she had witnessed? She shivered. What would she do if she did come face to face with him? She shook her head. It could not have happened that way. Vard couldn't have become the bear. It was the effects of shock and fatigue and all the events of the past days that had her seeing wild fancies.

"Daughter?" Prince Zialni stood, arms crossed over his chest, brows drawn into one thick black line.

Alecia pulled herself from her reverie and met her father's eyes. "Captain Anton was gravely wounded; even so he pursued the assassin into the forest when he fled. I believe he will die from his wounds." A sob erupted from her throat and a wave of hot anguish banished the chill inside her. Millie arrived at her elbow. "I ask leave to return to my room now, Father."

Prince Zialni bowed his acquiescence. Alecia curtsied to the king and queen, completely ignored Lord Finus and swept from the room. Millie scurried behind, babbling about the events of the night, but Alecia barely listened. Her mind raced as she tried to come to terms with what she had seen. The effect of the wine lingered and her head was still fuzzy. Millie helped her undress and tucked her into bed.

"I'll be here beside you in the chair, Princess. You close your eyes and all will seem better in the morning."

Alecia turned her head to the wall, away from the maid. No matter where her thoughts dwelled, she worried her life would never be happy again.

CHAPTER 14

THE brown bear lifted his muzzle from the ruined throat of the human, blood dripping from his whiskers. His shoulder and chest throbbed. This human had caused those hurts and the chase had been difficult. The bear didn't understand his compulsion to hunt and kill the man, just as he didn't know why he had spared the woman. Easy prey was the best, but she had smelled *familiar…* and that confused him.

He felt little desire to eat the flesh before him, but the energy expended had to be replaced and his wounds needed healing. He settled before the corpse, groaning as the strange hard objects that had pierced his body grated against bone, sending fresh agony into his chest and shoulder. He tasted his own blood. This human could provide the cure he needed.

One blow of his huge claw opened the chest wall. He seized the quivering heart and ripped it from the vessels that fed it. The organ disappeared in one mouthful. Blood pooled in the chest cavity and the bear drank from the fluid. Nature's healing energy flowed into him. He tore through the muscle that separated the chest from the abdomen and feasted on the liver and the spleen.

The bear knew he should be moving. Hunters would come, scouring the forest with their sharp metal, and he must hide until it was safe. A vague memory of the woman flashed through his mind again, but he didn't understand. The huge creature dragged himself from his resting place and padded off into the forest.

* * *

The buzz of activity downstairs awoke Alecia mid-morning. After lying sleepless for most of the night, she had fallen into an exhausted doze around dawn. Her mind swarmed with thoughts of Vard and the bear, her betrothal and the ball, skittering from subject to subject, not resting anywhere for long.

Eventually she had to acknowledge one truth. Vard was far from human. His transformation last night into a huge brown bear was not her imagination, and he had contemplated attacking her. Her survival had rested on the whim of a wild creature and, worse, that animal was her protector.

There was a knock on the door. Alecia ignored it and pulled the covers over her head. Perhaps whoever it was would go away.

"Princess Alecia, my dear," a smug male voice said from beside her bed.

Alecia sat up to find Lord Finus leaning over her, his eyes fixed to her bosom. "Why are you in my chambers?"

"Ah, my dear, you forget that I am your betrothed now. I can do *almost* anything I wish." His eyes roved over her face and shoulders and returned to the bodice of her nightgown. "I have come to inform you that King Beniel and Queen Adriana are about to depart. They wish to say goodbye."

Alecia stifled the impulse to order him from the room. She hated the way his eyes caressed her body, as if it were already his. "I thought they were to stay several days." It would have been better for Vard to kill her last night than to face the slow death of the spirit that Lord Finus would inflict upon her. She tried to tell herself that children would make her life bearable, but when she contemplated how those children would be conceived she felt physically ill.

"The events of last evening have unnerved the prince." A look of fury passed across the lord's visage. "He has decided that it will be safer for the king if he leaves now. I agree, even though it will mean the monarch misses our betrothal ceremony."

Alecia's stomach clenched at the mention of the ceremony but she refused to be distracted. "You look angry, my lord."

"I was frightened for your life, Princess. It is only natural. I could not forgive myself if you had been injured."

"You believe the bolts were meant for me?"

"What other conclusion could be drawn?"

"Surely Captain Anton was the target? He was, after all, the one injured." She drew her knees up beneath the covers and wrapped her arms around them. *Vard is out there somewhere, injured, perhaps dead. Vard is a bear!* Her whole being started to tremble and Finus didn't even notice.

"Regardless, Princess, we must assume it was an attempt on your life, and we must be more vigilant."

Finus's voice trailed away and his gaze narrowed, but what he saw in his mind's eye, Alecia could only guess. She was convinced that the attempt last night had been aimed at Vard. Had Finus ordered it? But why would he put her at risk like that, when a stray shot could have ended his plans to marry her? No, that didn't make sense either.

"Perhaps we shall learn more when Anton returns," he said.

Alecia drew a deep breath. "He's still missing? What of the assassin?"

"The soldiers found the mutilated body of a man in the forest this morning, just outside the grounds. There is no identification on the corpse but there was a ring on the body…" Finus's jaw looked so tight it was a wonder he could speak at all, "a ring bearing the serpent design of the guild of assassins." The lord seemed uncomfortable in the extreme and Alecia could well imagine her father had been harsh in his treatment of his future son-in-law. Perhaps Finus was not involved in the attack. After all, he had much to lose.

"The bear has not been located," Finus said, squaring his shoulders and peering down his nose at Alecia. Her betrothed had a truly remarkable ability to shrug off adversity. She could almost admire that. "Our tracker is still out. Perhaps he will find the animal and it can be killed. It would not do to have a man-eater roaming the countryside."

Alecia shivered. "You think the bear attacked the assassin?"

"There is no doubt, Princess. It seems the bear killed the man and then ate various organs. We must find the creature and kill it before it strikes again."

Alecia had gone cold. Her mind played the scene of Vard's transformation into the bear. She imagined the giant jaws tearing at human flesh and shuddered. It could so easily have been her flesh between those teeth.

"Princess, what shall I tell His Majesty?"

"What?" she said. "Oh, please ask him to wait. I will be down within the hour."

Lord Finus bent to kiss her cheek but Alecia turned away. His long fingers gripped her jaw and she gasped as cold lips descended on hers. She froze, terrified that he would push his claim right there in her room. The hard fingers left her jaw and trailed down her throat and breast. Alecia froze, unable to breathe, but just as she raised her hand to push him away, Finus straightened, cold triumph on his face. He left without another word and the tiny spark of hope left inside Alecia died.

* * *

King Beniel and Queen Adriana's entourage had assembled on the palace drive by the time Alecia dragged on a gown and made herself respectable. Ramón stepped from his position in the line of palace staff to escort her to the monarch's side. She refused to meet his eyes, still angry about his behaviour the previous evening.

Ramón leaned down to her and she stiffened. "I'm sorry for last night, Princess. It won't happen again, now that you are betrothed."

Alecia stared. "Your behaviour was inappropriate, betrothal or not!" she snapped.

He frowned. "It's just that I've waited so long for your love, Alecia. I couldn't wait longer."

"Be quiet," Alecia said. "This isn't the time or the place."

She swept a deep curtsy for the king and then the queen. "I'm distressed to see you depart so soon, Uncle… Aunt." Alecia could not find it in her heart to care. Her relatives supported her betrothal to

Lord Finus. She was truly alone. "Is there nothing I can say to delay your departure?"

King Beniel kissed her hand and then pulled her into his embrace. His breath held the faint odour of garlic, a fault she had not noticed when he had been the perfect uncle.

"My brother is right, my dear," said the King. "We cannot risk the life of our queen. We must take ourselves from this peril. By staying we further endanger your life and Jiseve's."

Queen Adriana stepped forward, resplendent in her cobalt-blue gown trimmed with gold lace. "All will be well, Alecia," she said, her voice low and eyes serious. "You will come to love your husband in time." She gave Alecia a brief hug. "Do not fight your fate."

Alecia's heart sank. The queen's words rang a death knell for Alecia's future happiness. Perhaps her aunt was also miserable? Alecia gave her another curtsy and stepped back. She could not forgive her aunt and uncle for supporting this union.

The royal couple looked at Alecia a moment longer, as if they wished to extend the conversation, then King Beniel ushered his queen into their coach. The royal conveyance rolled away down the drive to a blare of trumpets and a cheer from the prince's household. A few townsfolk also cheered and clapped from outside the palace gates.

Alecia trudged up the drive toward the palace steps. Ramón caught her up on the stairs.

"Congratulations again," he said. "You'll be busy planning the wedding now, I suppose."

"You think I'll be consulted on that?"

"What's the matter?"

"I don't see why I should accept this with good grace, especially in the company of friends," she said. "Lord Finus is the last man I would choose to marry. I hate him!"

"You knew yours would be an arranged marriage, Princess. You can't be surprised."

"I thought my father loved me enough to consult with me before choosing my husband. Then to pick a man almost old enough to be my grandfather…" Alecia shuddered.

"That's the way of many arranged marriages," Ramón said. "It's to be hoped that Finus still has it in him to produce the royal heir."

"No one understands! I'll kill myself before I let that old lecher touch me."

Ramón clutched her forearm. "You can't mean that!"

Alecia stared at him so he could be in no doubt of her sincerity. "I'll take my life, if I can. If not, he'll have to rape me to get me with child. Now, let me go."

Ramón released her arm but walked alongside her as she took the stairs to her chamber. "Let me guess whom you would rather wed," he said when they stopped at her door.

"I'm not going to have this conversation with you. I'm too tired."

"Have you heard that Captain Anton hasn't yet returned?"

Alecia swallowed a surge of panic at the mention of Vard. "I had heard. You didn't find any trace of him last evening when you entered the forest?"

"No. I soon realized there was nothing I could do until first light."

"What you did was foolhardy, Ramón. The captain wouldn't expect you to take a crossbow bolt for him."

Ramon's clear blue gaze clouded and sweat shone on his brow. "Your precious captain will have some sticky questions to answer when he does appear. Why he fled and left you alone, for instance."

Alecia knew Ramón well enough to see he was hiding something, but right at this moment she didn't care what it was. "I don't intend to stand in my doorway and gossip," she said. "If you have news of Vard – the captain – let me know. Please excuse me."

She closed her door in Ramón's face and leaned against it, taking deep breaths in the hope that she could bring the tide of her emotions under control. Tears wouldn't come but her entire body trembled. It had taken everything she had to hold herself in check as Ramón discussed

Vard. She couldn't abide it if he didn't return, or if the hunters brought word of the rogue bear's killing. Equally, Alecia didn't know if she could face the man who had awakened her. Her body yearned for his even now, but she was terrified of the animal that dwelled beneath his skin.

CHAPTER 15

VARD knelt in the shadows of the rain barrel and waited for the patrol to pass. He was loath to approach the witch but she was the only one who could help him now. He was weak, so weak. Dusk deepened the shadows. Just a few moments longer and it would be dark enough to reach her front door. There was no question of climbing in an upper-storey window in his condition.

He wondered what had occurred at the castle since the events of the previous night. A flash of Alecia's horrified face came to him and he drew a ragged breath. She had seen his transformation and he had contemplated attacking her. It could so easily have been *her* body he had ripped into last evening. The metallic taste in his mouth was testimony to the fact that he had drunk the blood and eaten the organs of a human. The foreign life force leaped through his veins, even as his stomach tightened at the forbidden meal. He might not know everything about the creature he was, but he knew that to feed from a human was taboo. What would the consequences be?

The hand that reached for the stone at his throat trembled. Perhaps it would've been best for him to lie down somewhere and die, but the time for that had passed. He could've made that choice last night and he'd not had the self-control. Now it was too late.

Alecia's face danced in his mind. She wouldn't come within a mile of him after what she'd witnessed.

That young woman was an itch he couldn't ignore. She stirred his blood, and it was not only sexual. He cared for her more than he should, more than was good for her. Theirs was a union that could never be, especially after her betrothal. Vard rolled his shoulders but the sharp stab of metal halted the move. Agony in his shoulder and gut made him sway and sudden bile claimed his throat. He sank to his hands and knees, panting away the pain.

Could he walk away from Alecia, knowing she had fallen victim to the intrigues of Prince Zialni and Lord Finus? She was brave, but could she deal with this betrayal by her father? Could she survive a loveless union with Finus? Vard didn't believe so.

The sun had set during his musings; he crossed the street and entered the alley that ran alongside the witch's residence. In moments he stood at her front door. He didn't knock but turned the knob, and the door swung inwards on silent hinges. As he crossed the threshold the hairs stood up on the back of his neck. Vard smiled. The witch's enchantments wouldn't stop the likes of him.

It was dark inside. He opened his senses to scan the surrounds. There were rats in the walls and a pulsating life force in the kitchen. He entered the short hallway that ran from the parlor and paused at the kitchen door. The old woman rocked in her chair by the fire, craggy features lit by the flames. She watched him, malice in her black eyes.

"You're not welcome here," she said. Her wild silver hair moved in the faint draught from the fire.

"I need your help. There's no one else."

"I know what you are." The witch stood and drew her tatty shawl around bony shoulders. One of her hands clutched something wrapped in cloth.

"I don't care what you know. I could expose you as easily as you could betray me. The prince hates witchcraft, so he'd take little convincing. And you've a connection to the mercenary murders. I know that for a fact."

The woman drew herself up until Vard swore he heard her ancient bones creak.

"I'm just an old healer, not a witch."

"The prince would be quick to condemn you. Are you willing to take that risk?"

"What would you do if I asked you to leave?"

Vard stared at the witch but neither his eyes nor his other senses could detect anything more than mild unease. "I can't leave," he said. "You must help me to return to the castle in full strength. The princess could be in danger."

Anger blazed from the old woman's dark eyes. "If you cared for Princess Alecia, you wouldn't have come back."

Vard tried to straighten and gasped as agony rocketed through his chest and shoulder.

"Don't fall now, you great lumbering oaf." She removed a heavy pan and a jar of something that looked like eyeballs from the table. "Lie yourself down here. My bones are too old to treat you on the floor."

Vard staggered across to the scrubbed wooden table and lay down on his back, his feet resting on a chair at the end. "What will you do, witch?"

The old woman had not moved toward him. "If you wish me to help you, stop referring to me as 'witch'. My name is Hetty."

Anger boiled through Vard. He felt like death and the old woman took offence at a name! He clawed at his composure and managed to bring his temper under control. "Forgive my discourtesy, Hetty. I'm not at my best."

"That may be true, Captain, but you're at *my* mercy." She pulled a knife from her sleeve and sliced Vard's tunic up the front then pulled both edges back to reveal his wounds. "A good thing you are not truly human. These wounds should have killed you."

"I realize that, woman! Why do you think I'm here?" Shock made Vard's voice harsh. The appearance of the knife had shaken him. He'd do well not to underestimate the witch.

Hetty glared and shoved a piece of wood in his mouth. "Bite on that. This will hurt." She plunged her fingers into the wound at his chest and agony blasted through his torso. Vard bit down hard on the wood to stop the scream that bubbled up. Moments seemed more like hours as Hetty's fingers probed the wound. What if the task was beyond her? Sweat broke out all over his body at the thought, but

Hetty smiled a grim smile, inserted slender silver tongs into his chest and pulled out the crossbow bolt. Vard couldn't avoid screaming this time, and the dark took him.

He awoke some time later and for a moment, didn't know where he was. Scant light from a fire to his left revealed jars of spiders, brains and other objects on a shelf and he remembered. Had he been wise to ask the witch woman for help? He felt across his chest and shoulder for the wounds left by the crossbow bolts. The injuries were still there but the pain much less. A quick glance through the window showed a faint lightening of the sky.

"You can get up when you feel strong enough," Hetty said, as she entered the kitchen, "and know how lucky you are. Those bolts went as close to killing you as a man ever wants to get to death."

Vard thought again that death might have been preferable, but then Alecia would be left to fend for herself. "My thanks. How can I repay you?"

"First threats and now gratitude! Well, you can thank me by getting on your way the moment you can put your boots on by yourself. Leave Brightcastle, Captain. I don't want you near the princess."

Vard wiggled his toes and discovered his boots had indeed been removed while he was unconscious. "You've a strong connection to her, Hetty. What is it?" He had a niggling in the back of his skull that wouldn't go away, and the witch's words had just stirred it up.

"I owe her a debt and that's all I'll say to the likes of you. Harm her and you'll answer to me."

A chill washed over Vard and he fought back a growl. It was time to test his strength before the witch lost her patience. He levered himself up. The tender flesh where the bolts had penetrated ached in protest.

"Get yourself home. I'm sure there's a scullery maid as will fix you a good hearty breakfast."

Vard pulled on his boots and Hetty ushered him to the back door. As he went to step into the alley, she grasped his arm. Her beady black eyes bored at him, the odour of mothballs and garlic swirling up his nostrils.

"Forget the mercenary murders," she said. "I know you killed the first man, even if the prince doesn't. Those men were guilty of their own blood crime: they killed the son of a farmer who wouldn't hand over more taxes. No one will weep over their deaths and Prince Zialni won't thank you for laying the culprit of the second murder at his feet."

Hetty pushed him from the doorway and slammed the door in his face. He stood for a moment, trying to understand the cryptic words. Then he laughed bitterly.

"Time to face the music," he said as he hugged the shadows back to the palace.

* * *

Alecia sat on the carved stone bench in the castle park, below the huge oak that held the hawk's nest. The odour of horse manure floated to her from the stables on the other side of the castle entrance. She didn't mind. It made a change from the stuffiness of her room. She sighed; she would have to dress for breakfast soon. It would be easy to hide herself away in her chambers, but that would enable her father to ignore the harm he inflicted upon her. She would present herself, head raised, like the princess she was, and she wouldn't cry in front of anyone.

Her stomach churned. There had been no word on Vard since the assassin's attack the night before last, but she would know if he were dead. The birds in the trees hopped from branch to branch, cooing softly as they prepared to greet the dawn. If only she could be as carefree. Their soft rustling ceased and Alecia scanned the shadows between the bushes for signs of a predator. She shivered, memories of the bear too fresh. Perhaps it was best to return to the castle now. She stood and found Vard ten paces from her.

His clothes were grubby and tattered, the tunic ripped right up the front. Black stubble covered his chin and dark shadows lay beneath his eyes. His gaze gripped her, the gilt specks in his irises mesmerising.

"Princess," he said. That was all, and yet she heard much in his tone that spoke of suffering and uncertainty.

"You shouldn't be here," she said. "My father has soldiers out searching for you …and the bear."

"I can explain."

"I don't want to hear anything you have to say. You can't convince me that I saw something other than what I did. I should tell my father."

"You have not?"

"I couldn't," she said. "You are free to answer his questions in whatever way you wish."

Vard took a step forward.

Alecia threw up a shaking hand to ward him off. "Stay where you are."

He flinched as though she had struck him. "Please, hear me out."

The pleading note in his voice speared her heart. Vard should never have to beg – not her proud captain. But he was also the bear. She nodded anyway.

"I'm a Defender, sworn to protect the innocent and the vulnerable. The bear is one of my forms, but one which I find difficult to control. When I told you someone had aided me in the darkest moments of my life, well…it was the bear he helped me control. I need to find another Defender who can teach me to master the bear…but that doesn't matter right now." He stepped forward again, but didn't touch her. His eyes reached out, scouring her soul, as if he sought to reassure himself that she cared. "You must understand, this gift, this curse…" His voice was bitter. "It's who I am. I have no choice…"

Alecia understood that last, the lack of choice, only too well. But then, there always *was* a choice if you were willing to sacrifice everything. What Vard asked her to do – to understand him, to forgive him for what he was; it was too much to ask.

She made her voice cold. "Leave me and return to your quarters. Present yourself to my father and he may take you back. I don't want to see you again." She watched Vard's eyes harden. It nearly broke her heart but she had to protect herself. Despite her fear, her body ached for his caress, her lips for his kiss. She closed her eyes to block his hurt from her gaze and took a deep breath, forcing the desire away. Instead, she pictured the bear as it loomed over her, as she embraced certain death. Alecia knew what he was now and she could not accept him. When her heart was steady and strong, she fixed her gaze upon the man who had been her protector. "Go."

He stared at her for a moment longer, and then stalked off into the bushes. She collapsed on the bench, trembling, and still the tears wouldn't come.

* * *

Vard stood before Prince Zialni, his chest bare to the gaze of the ruler, teeth clenched. Why did he put himself through this humiliation? He should have listened to his instincts and left the prince and his daughter to their fates. Instead, his concern for Alecia had brought him back – only to find that she despised him. Well, he had expected as much.

"You recover quickly, Captain. I have seen wounds like those kill a man and yet here you stand. What is your secret?"

"I've discovered much on my travels." Vard's short nails dug into his palms. "The forest holds many wonders for those who care to learn."

"You are telling me that this marvel was accomplished with leaves and spit?"

"It's more complicated than that, Your Highness. Suffice to say that certain remedies have aided my recovery. I was gravely injured, which is why I couldn't return sooner."

The prince stared at Vard. "You left my daughter in danger."

"I took two crossbow bolts for your daughter." Vard clung to self-control by a fingernail.

"You think the assassination attempt was aimed at the princess?"

"I think it wise to assume the worst until proven wrong."

Prince Zialni frowned and walked across the chamber to stand before the windows. "Perhaps you are right. Regardless, I am not content with your answers. Lord Finus wants you removed from the care of his betrothed and I am inclined to agree. You will vacate your chambers forthwith. Lieutenant Vorasava will take responsibility for the princess's safety. You will find the murderer who plagues Brightcastle Town. Vorasava has launched regular night patrols of the town and will advise you of any progress he has made. Be grateful; Lord Finus wanted you banished, however I have uses for you yet. See that you do not fail again."

The prince turned away. Vard gathered his shirt around him and strode from the chamber, his hand clutching the stone. On the threshold of his room, he stared at the marks he had carved in the door. Memories of that night crashed down on him. He was like a thistle seed, blown hither and thither by the wind, with no control over his life. Alecia held him in Brightcastle.

Knowledge crashed through him and he staggered against the door frame. *I love her!* His feelings didn't matter. Alecia needed him, and he'd been given the means to stay near her – or at least within reach. His changeling nature repulsed her but, he *would* watch over Alecia, no matter how she felt about him.

He stepped into the room and began to stuff clothes into his saddlebags.

* * *

Alecia was pacing her sitting room when there was a knock at the door and Lord Finus strode into the room.

"Princess Alecia," he said, "you look delightful." He took her hand and she flinched as his mouth brushed her fingers. "I came to advise you that Anton has returned. He has been relieved of his duties." He didn't let go of her hand.

"What do you mean?" Alecia could barely gather breath to speak.

"The captain is no longer responsible for your safety, Princess. I could not take the risk after he abandoned you. Lieutenant Vorasava will make a much more suitable protector."

"Where is the captain?"

Lord Finus drew Alecia to him, his eyes fixed on her mouth. "That is no concern of yours, my love. If I did not know better, I would think you had developed a fascination for the man. That would never do." He leaned closer until his lips brushed Alecia's neck. She could not hide the shudder this time and pressed her eyes shut, determined to ignore his lips as they worked their way from her earlobe down to the hollow at the base of her throat. This close, the odour of smoke on his breath made her stomach clench.

"Captivating." Finus still gripped her fingers and his other hand curled around her waist. Alecia trembled. If he chose to force himself on her, there was little she could do. Alecia doubted her father would protest if Finus bedded her before their wedding day. The prince was desperate to have an heir and, with the wedding to take place as soon as could be arranged, an early pregnancy would not be a problem.

"I cannot wait until we are man and wife, Alecia," Finus said, his pupils large with desire. "I feel your apprehension, my dear. All will be well once we are wed."

He leaned toward her and Alecia pushed against him, arching away. Anger leaped into his gaze. The arm around her waist tightened like an iron band. She hadn't known the scrawny lord had so great a strength. He pulled her against him and crushed her mouth beneath his. Alecia pushed at his chest with her free hand but Finus took his time over the kiss, his right hand running up into her hair to hold her head still. His mouth was so insistent that she couldn't draw breath to scream. After what seemed an age, Finus released her hair and pulled away. His arm remained around her waist.

"Do not think to fight me, Princess," he said, his voice cruel. "You are mine. You will show me the proper respect and affection as your betrothed, or I will come to your bed without the authority of the marriage vow. Your father would not object. I think he would turn a blind eye to just about anything. Compose yourself, my love. Our betrothal ceremony begins within the hour. See that you are not late."

He swept from the room, leaving her panting, the bile rising to her throat. She hated him and her father. She hated all men! Alecia crossed to the wood box and withdrew her favorite knife from its hiding place.

The sound of the blade moving across the whetstone as she sharpened it calmed her fears. She was not without choices.

The betrothal ceremony was over. The amethyst betrothal ring Finus had given her lay on the table beside her bed. Alecia fought down fury at the lord's choice of stone. The purple gem had been her favorite until now. *Will he destroy all that is dear to me?*

She stood before her mirror in dark gray tunic and leggings, smearing charcoal on her face. Her hair was tucked up under a black cap and a gray hood lay down her back. On her feet were soft leather boots.

Tonight, she would finish the job of killing the mercenaries, and if she were lucky, die in the struggle. She no longer cared. Lord Finus had made it clear how her life with him would be and she would rather be dead. Her father had watched the lord fondle her after the ceremony and barely frowned. With that level of discouragement, Finus would be even more likely to pursue his privileges as husband before the wedding took place.

Alecia had determined she wouldn't be there to suffer. She might as well do the world a service with her death and take as many mercenaries as she could with her. There was no one left to care about her, with the possible exception of Hetty. She gathered her weapons and left the chamber through the passage hidden behind the tapestry.

CHAPTER 16

ALECIA lay in the shadows across the cobbled road from The Dancing Lion. She had spied her three targets inside the tavern: the blond-haired man with the ruby in his ear, the heavy-set bald man with the bushy, black beard and the tall, thin brown-haired man. They were drinking heavily and pawing the serving girls. Easy prey, she told herself. Her first murder still haunted her, and not just because she had nearly died. The act had changed her; left scars that would never heal. She couldn't even contemplate going through with this unless she kept reminding herself that these men had killed Jorge. They deserved death. They *did*. And unlike the last time, Alecia would welcome death herself. Not caring about her own safety would give her an advantage, but all three men must die in the attack. She didn't plan on being around after tonight.

Several men had already left the inn but the mercenaries she sought were not among them. She tensed as three men staggered from the inn. Was one of them bald?

The men turned right and lurched into the street, their heels snapping on the cobbles. They were beyond drunk, and held each other upright. Alecia followed on the opposite side of the street, sticking to the shadows, her eyes glued to the men, heart pounding in her chest.

They passed a window where light spilled onto the street and she glimpsed a bald head and bushy beard. At least one of the three was a target, but she had to see if the others were as well. She continued on, her soft boots making no sound. The man furthest along the road tripped and pulled his companions down. Alecia saw the glint of a red stone as the man in the centre climbed to his feet and helped his friends up. The third man looked thin and exceptionally tall to her. It had to be them.

She slipped around the corner into the first alley she came to and pulled three arrows from her quiver. She stuck two head first into the dirt and nocked and drew the third. The men were dusting each other off and laughing over their stumble. She sighted on the chest of the tallest man, but as she prepared to loose the arrow, the clatter of hoofs rang in the street. Alecia withdrew further into the shadows as a troop of her father's soldiers trotted into view.

"Who goes there?" The leader shoved a flaming brand out to illuminate the faces of the three. "Ah, Raoult and your friends from the Lion. I would've thought you'd take more care, after the murders of those mercenaries last week." The torch allowed Alecia to be certain these were the three she targeted.

"We don't fear death, Sergeant," said the blond man with the ruby.

"Get to your homes and don't tarry, Raoult," the sergeant said, as he led his men past and up the street.

Alecia glared at the soldiers as they trotted out of sight, afraid she wouldn't get another opportunity to launch her attack. Contrary to Raoult's words the men peered around, seeming suddenly uneasy. Then Raoult slapped the bald one on the back.

"Don't fear, Dom, all will be well," he said. "Let's call on Silvandra. She'll take our minds from this grisly business." The other two laughed and they continued on up the street.

Alecia drew a deep breath. She could do this. These outlaws must be removed from Brightcastle Town before they raped this Silvandra, or worse.

She crept onto the street again and followed, half expecting to be accosted by some night prowler. Twice she thought she heard the clatter of the soldiers returning. No one came. Even drunk, the men moved too quickly for her to take aim in the darkness. Finally, they came to a crossroads and started down an alley. Alecia crossed the street and crouched in the deep shadow of a rain barrel. She rested for a moment against the wall, willing her heart to slow, her trembling to

still. It was no good, she couldn't achieve the calm she desired. *Ninny!*
You don't matter! Alecia turned her attention to her weapons, preparing
the bow and arrows as before.

The three men continued along the alley and pounded on a door
halfway along. After some moments, the door swung outwards. A
woman stood there in corset and knickers, with a flimsy robe draped
across her shoulders. Alecia stifled a gasp as Raoult pulled the woman
roughly against him. He planted his lips on hers and his free hand
grasped one of the whore's breasts. The woman struggled but Raoult's
two friends stepped forward and grabbed each of the woman's arms.

Alecia realized her hand was at her mouth and her eyes glued to the
scene. She took hold of herself, knelt and nocked her first arrow. She
aimed at the one called Dom, forcing her breath to slow. *Good enough!*
Her first arrow took him in the back and her next slammed into the
neck of the tall man. The bloodcurdling screams of the whore tore at
Alecia but she had the third arrow nocked before Raoult realized what
had happened. When he saw his friends dead at his feet, Raoult threw
the woman against her doorway and charged back up the alley.

Alecia crouched, paralysed as the mercenary thundered toward
her. She had no plan for this! With trembling hands, she dragged the
bowstring to her ear, sighted and released her third arrow.

In a heartbeat, Raoult was upon her. The arrow had taken him in
the right shoulder but his left fist glanced across her cheek and pain
crashed into her skull.

Blinking back the dark waves of fog that seeped into her brain,
Alecia struggled to fend off the clumsy blows that Raoult rained down
on her. She wriggled out from under him and began to crawl away, but
the blond man grasped her foot and hauled her back, his eyes striking
a chill through her.

"Kill me, would you lad?" Raoult's fingers closed around Alecia's
throat and squeezed. Her air supply was abruptly cut off and agony
rocketed through her as her windpipe was crushed. The mercenary's
smile slowly widened as she gasped and struggled for air, her fingernails
clawing at his hands, desperately seeking a weakness that would save

her. Raoult's face dimmed and Alecia slipped away, her last thought for Vard and the goodbye she had never uttered.

* * *

Vard strode down the darkened hall of the guardhouse, his mood sombre and his thoughts on the princess. Why couldn't he concentrate on the matter at hand? He had been called from his bed in the soldiers' barracks to interview a suspect. He should be glad there had been a development in the mercenary killings, but his chest and shoulder ached and the hour was late. No matter. His eyes would be enough to have the suspect spilling his guts, and then he could return for a much-needed rest.

The command sergeant who had summoned him stopped before a heavy wooden door bound by thick bands of iron. He raised the plank that secured the door and swung it outwards into the passage. The dark cell stank of wet straw, mould and mice. Vard's eyes went immediately to the form huddled in the corner.

"The lad was almost dead when we came upon them," the sergeant said. "I haven't had much from him since he woke up. Either he's scared witless or the strangling has done permanent harm." The man crossed the cell and lit the brand that sat in the bracket opposite the door. Then he gave the prisoner a kick on the shoulder. "See that you cooperate and it may be a quick death for you instead of crucifixion, boy." The captive whimpered and curled tighter into a ball.

"Leave us," Vard said.

"I'll be in the guardroom," the sergeant said as he left the cell.

Vard stared at the pathetic figure in the straw. The lad looked like the boy whom Vard had rescued from the mercenary. It seemed so long ago. Vague memories of the second mercenary death told him the prisoner was also a match for that killer. A faint smell of lavender came to him and he nodded. It made no sense that a lad would use perfume, but it fit with the fragrance he remembered. Now the boy had been accused of killing two more mercenaries and wounding another. He didn't seem capable of it.

"Look at me, lad," Vard said. "I think we've met before."

Vard's words only caused the boy to curl tighter into a ball.

"You've led me a merry chase and now it's time to put all to rights. You must pay for your deeds."

The figure in the straw raised a battered face. "My deeds!" the lad spat. "What of the foul deeds of those men!"

The vehement response shocked Vard. He knelt in the straw and peered at the prisoner. What had Hetty said? That the prince wouldn't thank him for finding the killer? "Who are you?"

The boy scrambled back against the stone wall, his eyes on the dirty straw. The fire had left him.

"I can't help you if you won't talk to me," Vard said.

The lad hunched his head further down into his hood and Vard lost patience. This was too much after being dragged from his bed. He reached over, grasped the hood and reefed it off the convict's head. Vard stared as long blonde hair tumbled down. "Princess!"

Alecia looked up at him her eyes huge in her dirty face.

How had he not guessed? All this time, the 'lad' had been right under his nose. His gaze took in the ugly bruises around her right eye and on her neck, and his heart lurched. She had almost been killed this night! But for the proximity of the sergeant's patrol, the princess would lie dead in an alley.

Vard reached out a hand to touch the bruise at Alecia's eye. She flinched at his contact.

"There is nothing you can do for me. Get up and walk away. I'll face the consequences of my actions, knowing I've avenged Jorge's death. You'll tell his parents that I've killed the murderers."

"You're making no sense. I can't leave you here. Tell the duty sergeant who you are. Your father won't allow you to hang for your crimes."

"Crucifixion is the sentence for murder. I accept it gladly, rather than the life sentence I already face."

"What life sentence?"

"What would you call it?" Her pupils were deep black pools and her fragile form trembled. Vard longed to reach out and draw her into his embrace. "Soon I'll belong to Lord Finus. I already do. He paws me like a village whore. I would rather die than let him take me. I would already be dead if my plan for tonight had gone as it should."

Vard drew a sharp breath. "You *wished* to die in the attempt on the mercenaries?"

"And now I must suffer crucifixion. I can't allow my father to find out. Better that I just disappear."

"Princess, you're not thinking. You can't keep up the charade through your trial, no matter how short it is. You must reveal your identity."

"And what then? My father will have to choose between enforcing my sentence and allowing me to walk free. His people will hate him, no matter his decision."

"His people already hate him. He's a bad ruler."

She remained silent while Vard's mind worked furiously to construct a solution. "I can't allow you to be punished for this," he said. "I'll go to the prince and confess to the killing."

Alecia surged to her knees and gripped his arms. "No, you must not do that. He'll somehow blame you for all the crimes and then order your death."

"And you wish to protect this man?"

"He is my father," she whispered.

As Vard crushed Alecia to his chest, her body shook as though she had a fever. He closed his eyes, willing her pain and fear away and finding an answering terror in his own soul. How had it come to this? How was he to haul her back from this precipice?

She pulled back, her eyes full of a new dread. "Take your hands from me. I don't know what you are, but you're not human."

Vard reeled as if she had thrown icy water over him. Slowly he let her go. "I don't care what you think of me," he said. "I won't allow you to carry this charade to its conclusion." He bent and gripped her upper arms and hauled her to her feet. "Cover your head."

Alecia's eyes contained more panic than he'd ever seen. Was she truly that frightened of him? His lip curled at the thought that he had ever imagined his life could be twined with hers. And he had, after the kiss they had shared and the moment in her chamber. He bent and retrieved her cap and hood from the straw and shoved them at her.

As if in a trance, Alecia fixed her hair, placed the cap on her head and drew the hood over the top. "Why did you protect me after the first mercenary died?"

Vard stared. He'd never known anything of this woman. "Instinct, the need to protect. I knew there had to be more to the attack."

"What do you mean by instinct?"

"I told you yesterday. At the very core of my being is the instinct of protection. I can't ignore that impulse when it strikes me. That day, I changed the details of the incident to protect you, even though I didn't know why at the time."

Alecia stared up at him, her scent confused and uncertain but less fearful than it had been.

He couldn't afford to hope. "Are you ready?"

"Tell me what you intend," she said. "I don't like the look in your eye." The words were defiant but the wobble at the end told the lie.

"You will follow me from this cell and back to the guardroom. Stay behind me so that the guards don't see you. If I say run, you'll do so and return to your father."

Alecia lifted her chin. "I will not."

Vard knew the stubbornness of the princess. This had to be good. "If I ever meant anything to you, do as I say. I'll hold the guards off as long as I can. I may pay with my life and am content to do this, but *you* must live. The kingdom needs you to be a force for good. Let that sustain you in the darkest times."

Vard paused to judge the effect of his words. Her eyes dropped to his mouth and she swayed toward him, but then stiffened and nodded. "It shall be as you say."

Vard pulled her to the door. "The passage is clear. Follow me."

He swept into the darkened hallway, keeping his cloak spread to provide more cover for her.

* * *

Alecia knew his scheme couldn't possibly fool the guards. They would see her and stop the escape. They could both die this night. Why hadn't she told him she loved him? He needed to know. Now it was too late. Vard swept along in front of her, his movements as graceful as a leopard, as dangerous as a wolf.

She struggled to keep up, her breath coming in gasps from her damaged throat. In moments, they reached the guardroom at the end of the passage and Vard strode in.

The duty sergeant sat at a sturdy wooden table, sharpening his knife on a stone. He looked up as Vard approached him. "Did the lad reveal anything, Captain?" His eyes widened as he caught sight of Alecia and he stood, his hand going to his sword. "Why have you removed the prisoner from his cell?"

"I thought to take him to another chamber," Vard said. "Surely you've one with… implements?"

The sergeant's eyebrows rose. "Torture has not yet been part of my duties. The lad will be questioned in his cell and nowhere else. The prince was very clear about that."

"Who's in charge of this investigation, man?" Vard said, his voice thick with menace. "Let me pass or you'll pay the cost."

"I've waited for the day I could test my skill against you." The sergeant's sword hissed from its scabbard. "The lad returns to his cell." He moved from behind the table, the tip of his blade pointed at Vard. Alecia moved away from Vard to give him room to fight then froze as the sergeant's eyes swung to her.

"Run, lad!" Vard said and hurled himself at the sergeant.

Swords rang as the two opponents came together. Vard launched a blistering attack but he seemed stiff, his usual deadly grace absent.

The sergeant easily met the assault and then countered with one of his own. To Alecia's eyes, Vard looked hard-pressed to hold off the attack. She had promised she'd run but instead watched in horror as the sergeant forced Vard past her and pinned him against the stone wall. Her eyes met Vard's, his glowing in the light of the guardroom. Alecia opened her mouth but no words came.

"Run!" Vard said again, desperation blazing from his eyes.

Alecia tore her gaze from his face and ran into the hallway. The passage sloped upwards, lit every ten paces by flaming torches. She hugged the rough stone walls, moving from shadow to shadow, and listening at crossing hallways before hurrying on.

When she was almost to the end of the hall, footsteps echoed from above. She looked around and spied a recessed doorway. In her dark clothes, it might provide enough cover to remain unseen. She slid into the niche and flattened herself against a rough wooden door. A fumble at the latch brought a squeal of protest from the metal. *Too noisy!* The footsteps had almost reached her. She would have to hide as she was.

Alecia closed her eyes, sure whoever passed would hear her thudding heart, and pressed her body against the moist stone. *Thank the Goddess for dark clothing and shadows!* The stench of male sweat filled the passageway as men passed, and she opened her eyes to see three burly soldiers approaching the guardroom. The clash of swords told her that Vard still fought. He wouldn't be able to handle four men; not in his condition.

She stepped from the alcove, her hand reaching inside her boot for her knife and finding nothing. *No!* Alecia crouched in the middle of the passage, imagining cold steel slicing through Vard with each ring of metal on metal. *Perhaps I could seize a sword from one of the soldiers.* It was not her preferred weapon, especially not in the close confines of the guardroom, but Vard needed her.

Then Alecia remembered why she had left in the first place. Vard would not be able to fight with her there. She would distract him when he needed all his attention to survive. Even with four opponents, he stood a better chance without her. A sob escaped her throat. *I can only help him by abandoning him.* If he died, it wouldn't be in vain. She stood, took a deep breath and ran up the passageway.

Alecia crouched in the shadows at the corner of the guardhouse, her arms clutched around her knees. She trembled so that her teeth chattered. Her heart had long since stopped its pounding and each beat sounded a dull thud in her ears; the sound of the nails being hammered into her coffin – or Vard's. She had to wait for him, or at least see his body carried out.

Seconds dragged like hours as she huddled there, the cold seeping into her fingers. The clash of steel sounded as if from a great distance and then the roar of an animal. The screams of men followed.

The realisation that Vard had shifted into the bear shook her out of her stupor and her heart soared. *He will be well!* The relief was short-lived. Cold memories of the beast sliced through her. In this form, Vard might destroy her. She must do as he urged and return to her father.

Pain shot through her head as she pushed herself to her feet. Staggering as if drunk, she kept to the shadows, thanking the Goddess that the guardhouse adjoined the castle grounds. She slipped between it and the wall that surrounded the castle.

A patrol of her father's soldiers surprised her as she stepped from the cover of the guardhouse. She flung herself behind a dung heap outside the stable, her hand pressed against her nose to stifle the choking fumes of the urine-drenched manure. The soldiers passed without seeing her and she hurried past the castle entrance around the corner to the trapdoor in a nearby stand of trees.

Her fingers grasped the metal ring concealed in the stone block and she heaved on it. The heavy stone wouldn't budge. Alecia collapsed, sobbing, her courage stolen by the violence she had endured and the injuries that made every muscle ache.

"Halt in the name of the prince!" a male voice said, close by.

Alecia flung herself over and froze as a sword tip hovered at her breast. The face at the end of the sword was Ramón's. She groaned. "I mean no harm. Leave me be."

Ramón raised the lantern he held, his handsome face suspicious. "Who are you and what is your purpose? This is a foul night to be abroad."

"Let me go, sir. I promise to go straight home."

Ramón's eyes narrowed and he bent closer, studying her face. Then he raised the sword and flicked the hood off her head, followed by her cap. Alecia flinched as her hair tumbled from its binding.

"Alecia!" He fell to his knees, dropping the sword and placing the lantern beside him on the ground. "You're hurt! Who has done this?" When she remained silent, Ramón made a closer study of her wounds and the clothes she wore. "It was you who killed those men tonight," he said. "It was you all along!"

Alecia was too tired to think of a convincing lie. She had no time to waste on Ramón when Vard might be right behind her. "I don't intend to sit here and explain myself to you. I'm the princess, remember? Let me go…now!"

"Oh no, Alecia. That's where you're wrong." His hand reached out to stroke the side of her face where a bruise throbbed. "I want to know everything." He leaned closer. She raised her hands to ward him off but he grabbed them and pulled her against him.

Panic fluttered in Alecia's stomach. She had been so close to safety and now Ramón might spoil everything.

His breath brushed her cheek. "I love you, Alecia. Your grubby little secret is safe with me. You belong to Lord Finus now, but he need never know. Let me be your first. Surely you would rather me than that old stork?"

"Please, Ramón, we're friends. Don't do this." Alecia could feel his tension, knew he wanted her despite the stench of her clothes. Perhaps what he felt for her really was true love if he could ignore that. She thought of Vard behind her and Lord Finus waiting for her back at the castle and shuddered. Let Ramón have her tonight. He would save her from the bear and she would give him what he longed for. At least Lord Finus would not get that gift.

Ramón must have seen something of her thoughts, for he bent and kissed her. His lips felt soft against hers and his arms moved around her, but his mouth didn't distract her as Vard's had. She found herself remembering another kiss, another embrace, and pushed him away. He sat back on his haunches, his hand gripping her fingers and a frown on his face.

"If you were ever my friend," she said, "help me lift this trapdoor and say nothing to my father."

"You'll grow to love me in time," he said. "Come away with me tonight."

"I know you care for me," Alecia said, "but I'm not for you."

"I love you," Ramón said. "There will never be anyone else for me. I've loved you from that first day when you asked me to fetch your horse and then complained when I helped you mount. I knew then that you were no ordinary princess. Your actions since have only strengthened my love."

"I can't discuss this here. It's not safe. I must return to my chambers and you to your room. Please, just help me with this door."

Ramón stared at her for a long moment and Alecia's heart ached at the disappointment in his eyes. Finally, he helped her to her feet, hauled the stone up and thrust the lantern at her. "Take this; you'll need it."

Alecia took the light. "Forget your feelings, Ramón. There can never be more than friendship between us."

"You considered more just moments ago," he said. "I saw it in your eyes."

"You saw hopelessness and desperation, not desire or love, and you deserve better." Alecia stepped down and didn't look back. She prayed that Ramón would return to his quarters. He was in danger if he was out this night.

The return to her room was accomplished quickly with the aid of the lantern. Flickering candles lit the chamber as she passed from behind the tapestry. Alecia built up the fire and sat on a chair near the flames, rocking back and forward, trapped in a limbo of uncertain grayness; her heart given to a man not human, but given all the same. Her promise to Vard had sealed her fate as wife to Finus and mother to his brats. Her dreams of being a warrior queen and of marrying for love would never be.

She tried to focus on the positives. All the mercenaries except one were dead. That would have to be enough to satisfy her need for revenge. She was safe – was that a positive when she had wished for death tonight? Vard was most likely safe as well, but she could not relish his life at the mercy of his animal side. She could choose a life for good, to balance the evil in her realm, but how much power would she have as wife to Lord Finus? He wouldn't be swayed by her desire for fairness and she couldn't continue to battle in a physical sense. Sooner or later, she would be found out.

Alecia stood and crossed to the mirror. *Holy Goddess!* The right side of her face was a mass of purple welts and scrapes, and her throat looked worse. A high-necked gown would hide some of the damage but there was little she could do about her face, unless she could reach Hetty. *Yes, that's the answer!* Alecia imagined traversing the darkened alleys again and the spark of hope inside her was replaced with violent tremors. She had no more courage left tonight. Perhaps if she took to her bed for a week, the bruising would have faded enough to hide with makeup.

She gave herself a sponge bath and washed her hair. Her clothes she tossed into the fire, the stench of burning dung infusing the room. Once her face was clean, she applied an ointment Hetty had given her for bruising. The flesh was so sore, she could barely bring herself to touch it, but she made herself rub in the ointment until her cheek throbbed and her stomach heaved. Then she applied the salve to the bruises that dotted the rest of her body, and donned her nightgown. She checked that her chamber door was locked, blew out the candles and climbed into bed. It was a long time before she fell asleep.

CHAPTER 17

AT midday the next day, an urgent knocking woke Alecia from an exhausted sleep. Pain seared her skull as she sat up in bed and a low moan escaped her lips. She collapsed back on the pillows. Her throat burned as she swallowed another moan. The knock came again, this time louder, more insistent. Gathering her courage, she levered herself up out of bed and walked slowly to the door.

"Who is it?" she croaked.

"Your betrothed, my dear. I wish to speak with you."

Alecia groaned inwardly. She cleared her throat, wincing at the pain the movement caused. "I can't see you today, my lord," she said. "I'm unwell. Perhaps tomorrow or the next day?"

"We need to discuss arrangements for our marriage ceremony, my dear."

"Whatever you decide will be acceptable," Alecia said. "You have impeccable taste." She imagined the garish decorations and extravagant ceremony that Finus would organise and almost opened the door. But she couldn't be seen yet. "I truly don't mind. You can tell me of your arrangements when I'm better."

"Very well, my dear," Finus said. "I will call again tomorrow."

Alecia heard him walk away and slumped against the door. She glanced in the mirror as she returned to her bed and gasped. The flesh had puffed up to close her right eye and the bruising was every shade of purple and blue. She found the ointment and forced herself to rub it into her skin again. *It's pointless.* Alecia slammed the jar back on her beauty shelf and gasped again as she saw a tray of food on her breakfast table. Even if her bruises had been against the pillow, any observant maid – let alone Millie – should have spied the damage to her face. It must have been Millie for she was the only person, besides Prince Zialni, who had a key. How long would it be before someone arrived asking her questions? Perhaps Finus already knew of her injuries.

She forced herself to eat as much of the food as she could. The porridge was cold but it slid down her tender throat more easily once it was mixed with honey and milk. There was crusty bread, which she avoided, a soft cheese and spiced wine. She sniffed the wine and then swallowed a mouthful. It warmed her stomach. Perhaps it would soothe her hurts and help her sleep. She finished the first goblet and poured another, which she finished too. Alecia returned to her bed and lay down with her damaged eye to the pillow. She was quickly asleep.

When Alecia awoke, it was dark. Some small noise had disturbed her. She froze, senses straining to detect anything out of the ordinary, and felt a presence beside her bed. A hand clasped her shoulder and she lurched upright. Her ruined throat strangled the scream that bubbled up.

"Do not fear, Daughter, it is only your father, come to see you. You've slept all day."

Alecia sighed with relief then remembered she couldn't let him see her face. "You…you startled me, Father," she said, her voice strained and her throat painful.

"You sound unwell, Alecia. What ails you?"

"I *am* unwell, Father, just as I told Lord Finus. Leave me be and I'll be recovered in a matter of days."

"Are you certain of that, Alecia?" The prince sounded tense.

"I'm sure it's nothing serious."

"I had Millie bring your evening meal. I will light some candles and talk with you while you eat."

"I'm not hungry, Father. I wish to sleep. Don't light the candles." Alecia's heart pounded at the thought of her father's face if he saw her injuries.

There was a long pause in which Alecia listened to the blood drubbing in her ears. Then her father's weight shifted from the bed and she sighed with relief. The next moment, her heart lurched as a glowing taper moved from the banked fire toward the candles on her bedside table. Light blossomed as he lit two candles. Alecia rolled over and buried her face in the pillow. She felt her father's weight on the bed once more.

"Leave me be," she groaned.

"I insist you look at me, Alecia," Prince Zialni said, his hand resting on her shoulder.

Alecia braced herself. When her father used that tone of voice, he couldn't be denied. She rolled over and sat up, her eyes slowly rising to his.

"Alecia!" he said, springing to his feet as if her face frightened him. "What has happened?"

"It's nothing, Father. A fall, nothing more."

The prince's eyes narrowed. "A fall did not do that to your neck." His fingers brushed the battered skin of her throat and he gasped and drew his hand away. "Who has…?" Alecia could see that he scrambled to understand the reason for her injuries. "I will kill him. I will kill whoever has dared to lay hands on you. Did they…?"

White-hot anger flared in Alecia's heart. "No, Father, my honor is intact," she spat. "But well might you kill the man who did this to me. He's already a murderer and I would be another to add to his tally if not for your soldiers."

Prince Zialni froze. "Murderer! What…?" Realisation dawned in his eyes. "It was you," he said. "*You* are the lad who has attacked my — the mercenaries."

Alecia went in for the kill. "They're your men to the core. You are ultimately responsible for Jorge's death."

"Jorge always did have more courage than brains," the prince said. "Is that what this is all about? You avenging Jorge's death?

"Yes," she spat, "and I'd do it again in a heartbeat."

The prince's face paled. "Are you mad? You could have been killed." Alecia tossed aside the covers and bounded from the bed to confront her father. "What will you do now? Hand me to the guards for crucifixion?" She should have stayed in her cell, refused to escape and made her father squirm. Well, he would suffer now, knowing that his actions had driven her to desperate acts.

He stared at her as if he had never seen the real Alecia. "Of course I won't hand you over, but how did you escape? The guards are all dead. There is blood everywhere and bear prints. I thought the prisoner had been taken by an animal."

"I wish I *had* died last night," she said. "That was my plan."

Her father's face went from pale to bright red in seconds. She had never seen him so angry. "Tell me how you escaped. If you were rescued, let me know who was responsible so that I can thank him."

"So you can kill him, you mean? You wouldn't want evidence of your daughter's crimes known by the populace."

The flush moved from the prince's face right down his neck as he gripped Alecia's arms above the elbow. "Do not taunt me," he said. "Captain Anton is again absent. Tell me he was not involved."

"*This*," Alecia pointed to her face and neck, "has nothing to do with the captain. What happened this night is about you and me." Pain and anger bubbled up until she felt her chest would burst. "I wish I were dead. You're no father of mine, to sell me off to Lord Finus. He's old enough to be my father, my *grand*father. He paws at me in your presence. Heaven forbid that I should have been soiled this night. Your precious deal with my betrothed would not have been honored then, would it, Father?"

"Your duty is to the kingdom, Alecia, as you have always known."

"You didn't even have the heart to choose a young man for me, someone I at least had a chance of growing to love."

"Do not be foolish. Finus brings alliances that I require. You will marry as soon as your wounds heal. And you will produce a son within the year."

"What do you think would happen if I presented myself to the lieutenant, Father?"

The prince's hands tightened on her arms. Didn't she have enough bruises without him adding to them?

"You will conceal your wounds until they heal. I will confine you to the lower cellar and tell Millie you have gone to the country for a holiday."

Alecia went cold from head to toe. "No!" She struggled against his hands, trying to reach him with her fists. "I won't let you cage me." She was too weak to struggle long. He gave her a small shove and Alecia toppled backwards onto the bed. She rolled onto her stomach, pain grabbing her face as it came into contact with the quilt. Her father's words came through a fog of hurt and exhaustion.

"You will do as I say. Your marriage will take place as soon as you are healed and Lord Finus will see to the matter of an heir for the kingdom. Get up and pack what you need. I will wait outside." Something on the bedside table caught his eye. "And you *will* wear that ring!"

The cold voice of the man she had believed would always love her squeezed the last ounce of hope from her heart.

* * *

Vard awoke in a shallow cave. Pain struck him from a dozen points as he moved. His tunic and breeches were filthy and bloodstained. He removed his clothes and examined the wounds one by one. None of them appeared serious – the benefit of injuries taken while in transformation. It was far harder to hurt a bear than a human.

Alecia was wrong. He *was* human.

He dressed and stepped warily from the cave where he had sought refuge the night of the assassin's attack. It lay deep in the forest to the north-east of Brightcastle. He stood at the entrance, as the first rays of the sun touched the tips of the trees beneath him. The peace of the scene contrasted with the tumult inside. There had been hard times in the past, not least being his early days of transformation, when he had not known what or who he was; the days after he had killed his cousin Frel. Then, as now, his lack of control over the transformation had almost been his undoing. He had thought those days of desperation were past.

Vard gripped the amber talisman and its warmth caressed his palm. He closed his eyes and Alecia's face came to mind; a face ravaged by bruises and fear. The face he had confronted last night. An ache began deep in his chest and grew in intensity. He squeezed his eyes tight and felt moisture on his cheeks.

"I can't bear this agony," he said, the words a whisper on the wind. He wasn't sure what the pain was, but he had his suspicions. It was an impossible situation. He had to leave before Alecia paid the ultimate price for his stupidity. Vard set off down the rocky slope, heading eastwards and away from Brightcastle.

He stopped at a stream at the base of the hill and drank deeply. The water refreshed him but when he went to wade across the stream, the ache in his chest returned. He tried to ignore it and within minutes, he could no longer walk. He crawled along on hands and knees until soon he couldn't even do that. Vard finally decided that he must return to the cave or die in the woods, and so he crossed back over the stream. Immediately the pain ceased. He shook his head, puzzled, and turned back to the east. This time the pain returned with just one step toward the water.

"I get the message," Vard muttered. He set off south and east, following the stream, unprepared to give in to the force that blocked his travel east. Each time he traveled further east than south, the throbbing in his chest crippled him. Eventually, he realized that whenever he took a course that led him away from Brightcastle, the pain would return. He was like a pigeon, and Brightcastle the coop.

So, something wouldn't let him leave Brightcastle. Was the force external or did it come from within? He couldn't leave, but how could he stay? He didn't remember all of the guardroom slaughter of last night but recalled enough to know that everyone had been killed. He'd sent Alecia away, but had she escaped? If she had returned, it was possible she'd been killed by one of the guards... or by the bear. *No!*

He'd remember that. He *would* remember Alecia. Suddenly he had to know that she lived.

Vard reached the outskirts of Brightcastle with the sun only halfway to its zenith. People were in the streets, going about their daily business. Children capered in the alleys and women in bonnets shopped at the street stalls. A thin man with a long moustache hammered nails to fix a notice on the front wall of a baker's shop. There were more of the same signs on several other buildings. He allowed a partial transformation to the hawk, just enough to take advantage of the bird's superior eyesight. What he saw made him slide back into the shadows of the alleyway.

As the transformation left him, Vard squatted in the dirt of the alley. So, the prince had a warrant out for his arrest. How much did Alecia's father know about the events of last evening? The notice claimed that Vard was wanted for treason and murder. It didn't mention the princess. He clung to the belief that Alecia would have been mentioned if she were dead. Would she keep Vard's secret?

It didn't matter if Alecia had revealed Vard's abilities to her father. The only thing that did matter was Alecia's safety. He'd discover her fate and then leave Brightcastle forever. Some other champion could save the populace from Prince Zialni. Vard climbed to his feet and set about securing a disguise.

Chapter 18

VARD opened the front door of the two-storey shack that lay in the heart of Brightcastle, ignoring the tingle that Hetty's warding spell always provoked. The filthy chimney-sweep costume had served him well, as had the soot covering his face. He'd walked freely through the streets to this residence but inside, he was unsure of his welcome.

He ghosted through the parlor and up the hallway to the kitchen. A glance through the doorway showed him the woman, seated on a stool by the fire and peering into the flames.

"That's a clever disguise, Captain," she said.

He leaped at the words, assuming the crouch of a street fighter, a knife with a chipped edge springing into his hand. *Damn the old witch!* How did she always manage to put him on edge?

Hetty cackled as she turned from the hearth. "No need for knives around old Hetty. You've nothing to fear…from me."

Vard slowly rose and replaced the knife in his belt. Hetty peered up at him as if short-sighted, but Vard knew there was nothing wrong with her vision. He couldn't detect an ounce of fear from her today; unlike the first time he had visited her. It irked him that the old witch could confront his powers with such equanimity. "Perhaps that's so."

"You're wounded again. Is that what brings you to my home?"

Vard frowned. First Hetty knew him without even looking, and next she discerned his injuries. Well, if she could tell those things, perhaps she could tell him what he needed to know. "My wounds are my business."

"It wasn't so last time," she said, her voice a harsh rasp. "If not for old Hetty you'd be dead meat, changeling."

A shiver ran through Vard at the memory of the healing that Hetty had worked on him only days ago. He didn't like to be reminded of it. "Something's happened," he said. "The princess may be in deep trouble."

"Princess Alecia *is* in deep trouble, but it's no concern of yours."

"The princess was behind the mercenary killings."

Hetty's eyes narrowed. "Rumor has it that the culprit died last night. Let that be an end to this sorry chapter."

Vard clutched the stone as rage ripped through him. "I must know if she lives! Don't play your games with me. She was gravely injured and held in prison. I must know if she escaped."

Hetty's dark eyes trapped Vard's and he felt a probing at his mind. He pushed against it, determined not to give in to her. Sweat oozed from his pores and the hairs stood on his arms. He couldn't be sure of the witch's power but if he died now, he'd never know if Alecia was safe.

"Don't be afraid. I'm not in the habit of killing men…or monsters." Hetty turned back to the fire. "The princess's wounds heal slowly."

"Then she's alive?" Vard knelt in front of the witch, hands bunched into fists, his eyes searching her craggy features. He almost flinched when her gaze snapped back to his.

"You truly are frightened for her."

"Answer me!" Vard said.

The old woman's dark eyes merely hardened. Vard had seen softer stares on street toughs. He swallowed his anger and took deep breaths to slow his racing heart.

"I said her wounds heal," Hetty said, "it's her spirit I fear for. Word tells that the princess has left Brightcastle, but my scrying doesn't support this."

Vard slumped in relief, his face buried in his hands. "Thank the Goddess. I feared she'd been killed after I freed her from the cell. I couldn't live with myself if I thought I had…"

"This is exactly what *I* feared," Hetty said. "You don't know what you do when you are the beast. What was it this time?"

"The bear," Vard said, his voice muffled through his fingers.

"You didn't even know if the princess survived."

Vard had no room in his mind for Hetty's scorn. Alecia had escaped the bear! His relief was short-lived as Hetty's words sank into his consciousness. "Left Brightcastle? What do you mean about scrying?"

Hetty folded her arms under her scrawny bosom and tilted her head to one side. She reminded him of a sparrow; or perhaps a raven would be a better match. "I have a talent," she said. "I can 'see' people I know, regardless of where they are. More clearly if I know them well. Mostly I use fire to do it, but water can be manipulated in the same way. With concentration, I can view those I've met, see whatever circumstances they find themselves in. It's easier if they're in danger or troubled."

Vard realized his hands were bunched into fists and he slowly relaxed them. Hetty's lips twitched as she watched him. "Show me Alecia...if you please," he said.

"What if I don't please?"

Vard leaned forward and reached for the woman but stopped himself before he touched her. She watched him, eyes narrowed, a smirk about her lips.

"You'd be wise not to lay hands upon me. I'm no use to you dead."

Vard rose and strode back to the doorway. Leaning on the doorjamb, he closed his eyes. The old woman knew how to get under his skin. He gripped the amber stone, seeking the void of the wolf's mind, the coldness and clarity, stopping himself on the verge of transformation. All would be well.

He opened his eyes and walked back to Hetty. "That should prove that I can control myself," he said. "I have to see her. Then I'll leave Brightcastle, never to return."

Hetty frowned. "An almighty effort in control that was. I'm somewhat impressed."

"You said you feared for her spirit. Why?"

"There is some dire threat she dreads. I've scried her twice in the fire. Her face... I haven't seen her like that before. She fears...herself. The ring Lord Finus gave her...she turns it round and round on her finger so that it has worn the skin away. I think the danger has to do with him."

"She promised me," Vard whispered.

"Promised what, Captain?"

"That she wouldn't hurt herself."

Hetty snorted. "Promises don't sustain us in the dark moments," she said. "I don't think she can bear this burden, whatever it is."

"She doesn't wish to marry Finus," Vard said. "She'd rather die."

Hetty's eyes widened and her hands gripped her apron. "I'll find some way to help her."

Vard took a step forward. "Don't be foolish, Hetty. I'll aid the princess. Show me her face. It might give me a clue."

Hetty nodded and beckoned Vard to the fire. He knelt beside her. The old woman reached her hand out and threw a green powder into the fire, muttering strange words.

"*Acthar scena morundi kabahl,*" she said.

The harsh accents sent a shiver through Vard. The flames swirled, tongues of fire twining around each other.

"*Findi behlal tedung mortunda.*"

Alecia's face appeared in the flames. She was somewhere dark and she stared unseeing, her hands clasped before her. Bruises covered the right side of her face and made a ring around her throat but it wasn't her injuries that caused Vard's breath to catch. He was unprepared for the despair that cloaked her form. As he watched, her hands moved and she began to twirl an elaborate amethyst band on her ring finger.

"The ring upsets her," Vard said. "Why doesn't she take it off?"

"Hush."

Vard glanced at the witch. She seemed entranced by the picture before her. Perhaps she channelled feeling as well as vision through the scrying. Whatever the truth, the old woman seemed almost as unaware of him as Alecia was of them. His eyes returned to the princess, searching for clues that would help him find her. She wasn't in her chambers. The small section of wall behind her was rough-hewn, even more so than the room he'd occupied when housed in the palace. Perhaps there was a cellar or dungeon?

If she were locked up, that would explain some of her despair.

The face in the flames disappeared and Hetty slumped on her chair. Vard reached out and steadied her. Her arms were skeletal beneath her dress.

"Take your hands from me," Hetty said. "I don't need your help." She shook his fingers from her and stood.

"Where was she?" Vard asked.

"In the palace." Hetty rubbed her arms as if chilled. "Somewhere cold, perhaps a dungeon. It was a close scrying. Sometimes I can discern mood and other hints, and this was one of those times. Princess Alecia is a prisoner in her own home. She has lost hope. I fear she'll do something foolish. There's no telling the treatment she suffers. I've heard rumors of how her betrothed touches her."

"Alecia told me as much that night in the cells. I can't leave her to his mercy."

"Leave her rescue to me, Captain. I don't trust you anywhere near her."

"You'll not be able to do what needs to be done. I'll go to the palace, find Alecia and bring her out."

Hetty stepped forward and pushed her craggy face up at Vard. "How many more times will you place the princess at risk?"

Hetty's words hit Vard and his determination faltered. "You're right. I can't trust myself around her."

The witch held out her hand. "Give me your amulet."

Vard frowned. "What has that to do with Alecia?"

"Just hand it over, changeling. I think I can help."

Alecia trusted Hetty; perhaps it was time he did as well. Slowly he removed the stone from the leather cord and handed it to the witch.

Hetty dropped the talisman into the pot over her fire, which immediately began to bubble. "Now, let's see. Oh yes. Claw of bear, feather of hawk and tooth of wolf, skin of human…" As Hetty listed ingredients, she dropped each one into the pot and as she did, noxious orange fumes swirled from the pot.

"Ferund moribun wolfin moria."

A sizzling began, building to a crescendo as the orange fog turned to red.

"Torbulen vico contrale verdu."

There was a popping sound and the crimson fumes settled, the sizzling died and the pot went quiet. Hetty hauled the mixture from the flames and removed Vard's talisman with wooden tongs. She lowered it into a bowl of water, dried it and held it out to him.

He frowned. "It's changed color. If you've destroyed it…"

"Place it around your neck," she snapped.

Vard threaded the leather thong back through the stone's setting and tied it in place. Had he been wrong to trust her? This stone was the only thing that augmented his control over his transformations. Lose that and he might as well kill himself.

Hetty regarded him with a knowing smile. "Test it."

Vard gripped the stone. Calm instantly enveloped him, a calm he'd never known. He stared at Hetty, who cackled out loud.

"Now the transformation."

Vard closed his eyes and sought the hawk, the ripple of feathers sprouting along his arms bringing memories of his first flight. He snapped back into human form and embraced the wolf, his fingers morphing into paws and his heightened senses already on the hunt for danger. He locked the wolf away and turned to Hetty, his heart lighter than it had been in weeks, years. "I've never had this control."

"The bear. You *must* master the bear."

Vard frowned but the witch raised her brows, not a trace of fear apparent. He closed his eyes again and morphed into the bear, revelling in the power and savagery of the beast. His limbs lengthened, shoulders expanded and the enormous strength of the bear flowed through him until he could contain no more. Vard held himself on the verge of complete transformation and then shut the brute away. *Just like that, with a thought, the beast is gone!*

"It works," he said, his words barely a whisper. "Thank you."

"Watch the amulet. When the color fades to amber, you must return to me and I'll renew the spell. Your search for a mentor must continue – for only he can bring you fully into your gift."

Vard froze, his heart thundering in his ears. He'd never told the witch of his search. "How did you know?"

"I've my secrets, Captain. I'll not reveal yours." Hetty pushed a large calico bag into his hands. By the smell, it contained bread and cheese. "Tell the princess I'll always come if she calls. I'll lend her strength, no matter what happens. You tell her that."

Vard nodded. "I'll find a way to get word to you of what transpires, Hetty." He turned and left the witch's house by the back door.

As Vard stepped into the alley behind Hetty's house he was seized by an almost overwhelming desire to storm the palace and rescue Alecia. Perhaps as the bear it would work, or perhaps not. His luck must run out sometime. He forced himself to head across town toward the forest and the cave that had provided refuge for him twice before.

CHAPTER 19

ALECIA jumped as the tray of food scraped across the rough wooden table just inside her door. It was the only way she had to tell the passage of the hours. The arrival of her three meals each day reassured her that time did still pass in the outside world. The two days of her imprisonment felt like weeks. She had nothing to look forward to, and her wedding to dread.

Her face was less painful today but her throat still ached when she swallowed. She had tried to starve herself, but her promise to Vard held her tighter than she would have imagined. She thought of him only fleetingly. There was too much pain down that path; the pain of loving and having that love choked by Vard's rejection; the fear of knowing that he wasn't human and that their lives couldn't be shared.

But Alecia couldn't subdue all of her feelings. At times, her desire for Vard rose up within her and she allowed memories of his hands on her body to heat her blood. Even now, her pulse quickened at the thought of his lips and the hard strength of his arms. As she battled with the need to surrender to her desire, someone cleared his throat by the door. She rolled over on her bed but it was too dim to see anyone.

"Father?" She sat up and pushed her hair from her face. Perhaps he had changed his mind. Perhaps he too remembered the times he had read her bedtime stories and taken her for picnics, just the two of them. They could still repair their fractured relationship.

"It is your betrothed, Alecia dear," the hated voice said.

Cold settled in her gut. She froze, unable to speak, as Lord Finus came to her bedside. His hand gripped her chin, turning her head this way and that.

174

"Come, Alecia, you heal too slowly." He dropped his hand from her face and sat on the edge of the bed.

Alecia leaned backwards until her spine rested against the bed head.

Lord Finus placed one hand either side of Alecia's legs and swayed toward her, his eyes on her mouth. "I am anxious for us to begin our life together." He wrinkled his nose. "I will have water and a tub sent so you can bathe." His left hand caressed her throat and Alecia gasped as it slid downwards to cup her breast through the fabric of her nightgown. His thumb caressed her nipple and she managed to free her hand enough to slap his face. He laughed. "I like my women with a bit of fight." He secured her arm and returned his attention to her nipple. Every muscle in her body tightened in revulsion.

Finus stood and leaned over her, his cold mouth capturing hers. Alecia couldn't move. She had no alternative but to wait until he had finished with her. The lord's hand slid behind her head and his kiss deepened. His tongue probed her mouth. Alecia tried to push him away but one hand held her while his other hand left her hair, tugged on the ribbon that gathered the neck of her bodice, then plunged inside the material to squeeze her breast. His lips left hers and moved to the line of her jaw and then leisurely down her throat.

Shuddering with revulsion, she wrenched her hands free but he recaptured them in both of his and forced them down either side of her. *He is so strong!* Her breast was bared in the struggle and Finus licked the nipple, his tongue encircling the delicate tissue. Alecia flung her head and body to the side, trying to wrench her breast from his mouth. "I don't want this."

"It is mere days until our nuptials, my dear," Lord Finus said. "I can feel your desire. I knew you would warm to me. Am I not a considerate lover?" He lay fully on top of her, his bulging manhood thrusting into her belly. "No one will disturb us, beloved. You cannot refuse me now." His lips returned to her mouth as he released her hand and hauled the skirt of her nightgown toward her waist then grasped her pantaloons. Alecia writhed under him, clutching at her undergarments. *He will rape me!*

"Take your hands from the princess," a voice said from the doorway.

Lord Finus tore his mouth from hers and rose from the bed to face the intruder. Alecia collapsed against the pillows, panting, and shoved her skirts down to cover herself. A tall woman in an ill-fitting servant's dress stood in the shadows. The bodice strained across her shoulders but was not filled at the chest, and the skirt was too short. A sword belt hung from her waist and she wore boots.

Finus drew himself up to his full height. "Leave us, woman."

The servant stepped forward, sword in hand, and Finus gasped. "You!" His weapon flew from its scabbard as he stepped away from the bed.

Alecia stared at the swords and then at the woman. There was something wrong… "Vard!" In other circumstances, she would have laughed out loud at the sight of the powerfully built captain in a maid's dress. Wherever had he found one that would even half fit him? She pulled her bodice up over her breasts and leaped off the bed, hauling her pantaloons back up beneath her skirts. "You shouldn't be here." He had come for her! He did care. Perhaps…

Vard's eyes flickered toward her and back to Finus. "I begin to wonder at the wisdom of my actions, Princess," he said, his voice tight. "I believed you to be prisoner here." The two men circled each other.

The disgust in his eyes cut Alecia to the core. How must it appear to Vard? That she welcomed the attentions of her slimy fiancé? Anger surged in her, giving her strength. "I *am* a prisoner, but it's my lot to bear, not yours. Please go before you are captured."

Vard grinned, but there was no mirth, only mockery. "I'd need to fight my way out in any case. Somehow I don't think your betrothed will allow me to leave."

Finus snarled and launched himself at Vard. Their swords clashed, sending sparks into the dimness. Alecia retreated to the corner of the room, her eyes unable to leave the two men as they fought for her. The dress encumbered Vard, its skirts threatening to trap the sword. Twice, Alecia believed he couldn't recover and both times, Vard's sword jerked free of its entanglement and blocked savage blows from Finus. Her betrothed was a skilled swordsman, a fact that Alecia had not known, and Vard seemed the underdog with the handicap of his disguise.

Alecia's fear grew, both for Vard and herself. He had come to rescue her and it could very well be his undoing. She dared not examine how his death would cripple her heart, because her feelings for Vard were based on a lie. He wasn't human. Besides that, Vard had seen her with Lord Finus and thought that she welcomed the lord's attentions. He wouldn't want her now, even if she still craved his love. Oh! She hardly knew what to think!

As she watched, Alecia became aware that Vard was luring his opponent away from her. Her hopes rose as he appeared to lull her betrothed into a false sense of confidence. Vard repeatedly fell back, seeming exhausted, and then would rally only to be pushed back again. Finus's face was triumphant, as though victory was assured. As Vard fell to one knee, the lord charged him, his sword centred on his opponent's heart.

Alecia's own heart hammered and her stomach had tied itself into knots. She didn't want to see, but couldn't take her eyes from Vard as Finus loomed over him. At the last second, Vard spun on the ball of his grounded foot and slid out of the path of Finus's sword, his own weapon striking home as the lord's attack carried him past.

Now it was her betrothed's turn to collapse to one knee. The sword fell from his hand and Alecia watched blood drip onto the stones from a wound in the lord's side. Vard pushed himself upright and stood over the injured man, his breath coming in gulps. Perhaps he had been as hard-pressed as it appeared.

Finus's ashen face sneered up at Vard. "Finish me off," he said.

A muscle along Vard's jaw tensed. "Your fate is sealed, my lord. Already the Goddess calls to you. I don't have to act."

Alecia stepped forward until she stood beside the two men. "He needs help."

Vard looked at her then, contempt in his gaze. "Have things changed so much, Princess, that you now care for this man? You once told me he was the root of all your suffering and that of the kingdom. Does he now deserve your love? Have his hands awakened your desire?"

Alecia dropped her eyes before his derision, the hot flush of shame flooding her. Finus had slumped to the floor, hand gripping his side and eyes half-closed. His breathing rasped in the quiet of the chamber.

"You don't understand," she said, tears spilling down her cheeks. What matter her dignity when Vard hated her? He thought her easy prey for any man – him, Ramón, Lord Finus. A sob rose in her throat and she swallowed it down.

"I understand what I saw." Vard grasped her shoulders so that she had to look at him. "Your betrothed is dying. Make your choice. We must leave now or be caught." His eyes trapped hers, the gold flecks threatening to engulf the green.

Alecia fought for breath.

"Will you come with me or stay?" he asked.

Alecia shook his hands from her shoulders and braved the contempt in Vard's gaze. "A choice, you say. Stay or go. I know what I face if I stay. What if I go? Will you care for me as my father will? Or a husband?" She realized what she might be asking, and couldn't help the gasp that escaped from her throat.

Vard's eyes hardened further. "I hear footsteps." He stepped past Finus and strode to the door. As Alecia watched, Vard poked his head into the hallway and disappeared into the darkness.

Alecia took a moment to allow her options to sink in. She contemplated staying in Brightcastle. Vard clearly didn't love her, even though his body was the one she craved. But if she stayed, there would be more occasions like this. She couldn't trust her father.

She sighed, slid the amethyst ring from her finger and laid it on the lord's chest. As she stepped into the hall, strong arms enveloped her and a hand clamped over her mouth.

"Quiet," Vard whispered in her ear. He released her but kept hold of her hand and drew her along the hallway. Boots thudded on stone and Vard pulled Alecia through a door just in time to avoid two men.

"The lieutenant and his lackey," Vard whispered as he peered through the crack in the door.

Alecia didn't understand how he could see anything in the dark, but when he looked at her his pupils glowed. She shivered. Vard's vision might be as good as any creature of the night. He wouldn't hurt her; he just would not.

A scream cut through the relative quiet of the room behind them and Alecia leaped forward, slamming into Vard. He muffled an oath and pulled Alecia back into the hallway as a cry of "Thief, thief!" screeched from the throat of the woman whose bedroom they had invaded. Alecia's courage faltered. They would be found and Vard crucified for murder.

His hand squeezed hers. "Don't lose hope."

They continued along the passage to an intersecting hall that led to the entrance of the castle. Vard stuck his head around the corner. His eyes found hers. "It's guarded."

"Foul murder! Intruder!" Cries came from the direction of the cellar.

"If you've any ideas, Princess," Vard muttered, "now would be the time to tell me."

Alecia met his eyes and swallowed. "We're in the east wing. There are hidden passageways. One of the access points is in Ramón's room. It will take us outside."

"Lead the way," Vard said.

Alecia turned back along the hall and took the passage that led to the kitchens. Halfway along, she pulled Vard into a narrow alcove that immediately became a staircase. It was used by the servants for access to the guest chambers. Vard pushed past, Alecia stumbling up the stairs behind him. At the top, they paused. Vard peered into the broad hallway that serviced the guest rooms.

Alecia stuck her head below his and pointed to a room across the hall. "That's Ramón's," she said. Dim light showed under the door. "Please hold your tongue with Ramón. Allow me to speak and he may help us."

He shrugged and pulled her across the hall and through the door, closing it quietly behind them.

Ramón had just risen from his bed. Alecia's eyes widened at the sight of him. He yelped and drew a blanket around his nakedness. "You!" he said, as he recognized Vard. He reached for his sword, which stood propped against the wall near the bed, and in seconds, it lay at Vard's throat. The captain hadn't made a move. He stood defenceless, his sword still sheathed. Ramón eyed Vard's disguise and a smirk appeared on his face. "Not much of a man now, are you? Move away, Princess."

Alecia stepped in front of Vard and placed a hand on Ramón's sword arm. "Let us go. In the name of our friendship, please let us go."

"Let this clown escape and lose my head, you mean? Some of us have to live here." Ramón's sword hand moved forward an inch. Alecia heard a sharp intake of breath behind her.

"No one need know, Ramón. There is access to a secret passage in this room." Alecia pointed at the tapestry of the dragon. "The entrance is behind that wall hanging. Let us through and lead the search away from the exit. That's all I ask."

Ramón stared at her, his knuckles white on the sword hilt, his other hand grasping the blanket that wrapped his lower body. "All you ask! It's too much."

"Please, Ramón."

His eyes moved to Vard, anger bordering on hate clouding his gaze.

She was asking a lot. Would it prove too much? "He's my only chance of a life. You know what awaits me if I stay."

Ramón's eyes flicked back to hers, all the love and pity he felt for her evident. Alecia's heart ached at the wretched situation.

"What has he done?" Ramón asked. "Other than let the prisoner escape." His eyes didn't quite meet hers. "What foul deed has he committed this night?"

Alecia frowned. Would it help or hinder to answer that question? "Finus and Captain Anton fought. My betrothed took liberties he should not have…" She found she couldn't go on.

Ramón grasped her hand and the blanket covering his nudity fell away. He didn't seem to notice. "I'm sorry, Alecia. Don't talk if it pains you. I take it the lord is dead?"

Alecia shook her head. "I don't know. He was gravely wounded. I never wished for his death."

Ramón hugged her to his chest in a brief squeeze while Alecia tried to erase the image of his naked body from her mind. What must Vard be thinking?

The squire released her, still standing without cover. "Alecia, with Finus dead, don't you think our union might stand a chance?"

Vard growled and Alecia tightened her grip on Ramón's sword arm. She glanced over her shoulder. Vard's eyes held a feral sheen. A trickle of blood slid down his throat from the point of the sword.

Alecia looked back at Ramón. "My father would never allow it. You know that. Any hope on your part is baseless. I've already told you, there's a girl out there who will love you utterly and completely. Just let us go."

She felt Ramón's grip on the sword tighten and she tensed, ready to stop him from running Vard through. Then the sword dropped.

"Cover yourself, man," Vard said, sounding more angered by the squire's lack of clothes than by his near miss.

Even in the dim light, Alecia watched a slow blush stain Ramón's cheeks. He handed Alecia the sword and pulled on a pair of breeches that lay on the floor. She couldn't help admiring the smooth lines of his thighs and buttocks. Ramón retrieved his sword from Alecia before handing her a candle from his bedside. "Take this and go," he said, "before I change my mind."

Alecia took the candle and grabbed Vard's sleeve to pull him with her, but the stubborn man didn't move.

"I won't forget your help, Zorba," he said and held out his hand.

Ramón ignored the hand. "Go and beware, Anton. The next time I see you, Alecia may not be there to stay my hand."

Alecia tugged at Vard who just stared at Ramón. If only he could keep his temper…

There was a noise outside in the hall and Alecia pulled on Vard's arm again. "They're coming."

Vard turned and followed her to the tapestry of the dragon. He held it aside while Alecia raised the candle, searching the wall for the hidden latch that would open the passage. Doors along the hallway crashed open. They must be searching this floor! *There!* She pulled the concealed lever and a section of wall moved with a loud squeal. Alecia tried to step through but Vard was there before her. He disappeared into the dim passage and Alecia followed him.

"Thank you, Ramón," she said and pulled the lever that would close the door. She caught one last glimpse of his forlorn face as the tapestry fell back into place.

Alecia hesitated, struck by the enormity of what she was doing. She was abandoning everything she knew. Yes, she was running from a cruel father and a miserable life, but what future could Vard offer? Perhaps he cared for her, though clearly his respect had diminished after the events of this night. Her heart shrank at the thought of how he must regard her now. If only she had fought Lord Finus harder; been able to stop his wandering hands. And what of the beast that lurked within Vard? How could she think of stepping into the night with him?

Vard faced her. "It's too late for doubts now."

"I know. It doesn't make this easier." She straightened her shoulders and met his eye. "Lead on."

The passage was dark despite the candle, and the trip to the stairs that led to the trapdoor outside the castle grounds was perhaps three times longer than she was used to. This part of the passageway had not been used in a long time and the tacky strands of cobwebs grabbed at her as she passed, even with Vard leading, brushing them away.

Finally, they arrived at the stairs that led up to the trapdoor. Vard surprised Alecia when he undid his sword belt and pulled the servant's dress from his body so that he stood in his boots and all-too-revealing hose. She knew she shouldn't stare, but her arm raised the candle of its own volition, painting Vard's glorious body in burnished russets and golden hues. If she had admired Ramón, Vard's form pushed all thought from her head.

"The dress encumbers me and we can't risk anything slowing us down," he said, taking in her rapt attention. "My clothes are hidden in the park. You'll excuse my undress?"

Alecia's eyebrows shot upwards. "Excuse?" No other words came to mind. Jumbled thoughts played leapfrog over one another in her brain. She struggled to sort them, her eyes drinking in every line and plane of his form; she was mesmerized by this half-naked man and yet nervous of being alone with him.

He frowned at her and slung his sword and belt over his shoulder. She admired his thighs and buttocks as he climbed the stairs; the way his broad shoulders and muscled arms heaved the trapdoor upwards. Dust sifted from the ceiling as the door banged on the stone above and he disappeared.

His head reappeared seconds later. "All clear," he said. "Climb the stairs and snuff the candle before you exit."

Alecia did as she was told and Vard helped her out before lowering the trapdoor into place. He grasped her hand and moved off toward the trees that signalled the beginning of the forest. The darkness now hid his form from her but Alecia didn't need vision when she had imagination. She berated herself for her distraction when the danger was so great.

Vard led her straight to a pile of clothes and Alecia marvelled at his ability to find his things in the dark. Then she remembered that he must have been able to track them by smell and felt the familiar tightening of her stomach. It was cowardly to fear this side of him, but she couldn't alter her reaction to the beast within.

There came thuds and a rustling as Vard removed his boots and donned the clothes he had left there. Howling eddied from the direction of the castle and Alecia looked over her shoulder. Lights bobbed toward them.

"They've loosed the dogs," Vard said, his voice muffled as he drew his shirt over his head. "I feared Zorba would betray us."

Alecia frowned in the darkness. "He would not!"

"He hasn't given up on you, Princess. He deludes himself that he can have a future with you. Of course he'd betray you if he thought he could get rid of me and raise his standing in your father's eyes. It's a good plan."

"Except I've told him we have no future," Alecia hissed through her teeth. "My father would never allow it."

"We've no time to stand debating." Vard grasped her hand and pulled her after him into the trees.

Wounds and days of confinement had sapped Alecia's strength and she was no match for Vard, or those who followed. The dogs and horses were gaining ground and the only thing that kept her moving forward was Vard's grip on her fingers. Finally, chest burning, she pulled her hand from his. A fit of coughing shook her. "I can't go on," she gasped. "Leave me here and I'll face them."

His hand grasped her shoulder. "I *will* see you to safety, whatever happens. Now come!"

"I can't, truly. Don't sacrifice yourself for me. Go!"

Alecia thought she heard Vard grind his teeth. "There's a way out, if you dare," he said.

"What?" She wasn't sure she wished to hear, by the tone of his voice.

"You know what I am. As the wolf, I can carry you, and the dogs will be less eager to follow. Horses also hate wolves. You'll have nothing to fear."

Alecia stared, her thoughts frozen. "Wolf? I thought… you are the bear. How can you also be a wolf?" In the midst of her shock, anger flared. *Will I ever truly know him?*

Vard's hands caught hers. "They're almost upon us. I have three animal forms, but we don't have time to talk now."

"You should've told me about the wolf, about all of it!" So much made sense now; his horse's fear, his uncanny grace of movement.

"Would it have made you feel any better?" His words were ground out, his fingers tight around hers. "Your decision, Princess."

"Will I be safe?" Could she ride a creature that might tear her to shreds in a heartbeat?

"I believe so." Vard squeezed her fingers.

In that moment, she loved him for giving her time, for not rushing her. But what choice did she have?

The barking of the dogs gained intensity as a gust of wind buffeted them. She saw the lights of torches through the trees. Alecia closed her eyes, reaching inside for strength. "Go ahead," she said. "Do what you must."

Heat bloomed beside her and she reached out her hands toward the warmth. Her fingertips encountered soft fur. A deep growl rumbled at her touch and she snatched her hands back. A cold, wet nose brushed against her face and a tongue licked her cheek. Her intake of breath caused another growl, but a large shaggy body shoved against her. Could she trust him?

She must. Alecia reached out again and felt along the wolf's neck until she came to the shoulders. She took a deep breath and vaulted onto its back, onto *his* back.

"It's Vard," she said to herself. "It's only Vard. All will be well."

The huge wolf bounded away, the gait like that of a horse, only smoother. The powerful muscles of his limbs bunched and stretched beneath her. She clutched his long hackles and gripped with her knees, becoming one with the wolf. Sounds of pursuit fell away as they raced through the woodland and entered the denser forest that lay north of Brightcastle. The wolf stopped once for a drink at a stream and Alecia strained her ears for sounds of pursuit, but the wind in the trees and her racing heart were all she heard. When they continued, they splashed in the shallows for some distance before gaining the bank once again.

Finally, when she felt she couldn't hold on for another minute and her body was slumped with exhaustion, her mount stopped. He whined. Alecia didn't need any further invitation to slide to the ground. Her legs folded under her and she sat on the damp earth. It was too dark to see her surroundings but she sensed Vard pad away and crawled after him. She could have been crawling over a precipice, but Vard's low whines kept her shuffling forward until she felt dry dirt under her fingers.

The air was cold here but the wind had died. She shivered. Where had he taken her? The panting of the wolf sounded a few paces away. He whined once more. What would he do now that the danger was over? Would he remember her? As she sat, her fingers fell upon the rough cloth of a sack. She drew it into her lap and hugged the bag to her. They appeared to be in a cave, the entrance to which was outlined by the creeping light of a new day. When she looked in Vard's direction she could make out the huge form of the wolf. He licked his pads, his eyes flickering to her uneasily.

The cave continued to lighten and Alecia was able to see the magnificent creature that had rescued her. He was massive, the largest wolf she had ever seen. His thick pelt was a dark gray with lighter belly hair, and his feet were the size of small dinner plates. Golden eyes watched unblinking, glowing softly, as Alecia shuffled back against the opposite wall of the cave. It was foolish to stare but she couldn't take her eyes from him.

The wolf bounded to his feet and let out a whimper. Alecia yelped too and flattened herself against the rock wall. The wolf padded toward her, eyes fixed on hers. She had no weapon if he decided to attack and even with one, she would have felt as helpless as a babe. Those eyes were mesmerising; the pink tongue licked the black lips and the mouth opened to reveal fearsome teeth, much larger than a dog's. In seconds, the wolf stood close enough that his hot breath brushed her cheek. He stared for a moment then lay down, his belly facing her. He whined again and began to lick his feet. Bloody gashes marred the pads of three paws.

"I'm sorry you suffered for me, Vard," she whispered. She put her hand out and rubbed the side of his chest. The wolf went on licking the pad of his front foot, and as Alecia became more confident in her stroking, the wolf sighed and lay back, eyes closed.

She smiled and shuffled closer to the beast that was Vard, finally laying her head on his shoulder. He was so soft and Alecia was exhausted.

In moments, she fell asleep in the warm embrace of her rescuer.

CHAPTER 20

WHEN Vard awoke, he was himself again; the human who was not quite human. The sharp pain of loss hit him, and fear at feeling the loss. That hadn't happened before. His only teacher had warned him that, with each transformation, he'd lose a little of his human self and become more animal. The trouble was that Vard could phase into three different creatures. Which one would he ultimately become and how long would it take? Could the change be slowed or halted? The time had come to find the answers.

His eyes fell on the sleeping woman beside him and his unease grew. Images of her being ravished by Lord Finus flashed into his mind. Disgust gripped his stomach and he shook his head. The Alecia he admired wouldn't allow her body to be molested by one she hated, at least not without a fight. Would she?

He pushed down his anger and examined the princess again. Even in her nightgown, with her hair full of twigs, she was beautiful to him. He'd never before realized how beautiful. Much of that loveliness came from her bravery, her spirit. Alecia had forced her way into his heart in the past weeks, but she couldn't stay with him. She wouldn't want to. His chest ached at the thought. He wanted her to need him; wanted her to want him. The heat in his belly grew. He wanted to possess her.

Vard stopped himself, breathing slowly and drawing on the core of calm within the stone for aid. Alecia had the courage of a lion. No woman he'd known could have endured what she had and survived. She deserved so much more than this – a filthy cave in a forest and a changeling for company.

He pushed himself up, groaning as aches and pains made themselves felt. His feet were agony. They alone should force him to stay in this cave for days yet. He didn't have days.

Vard pulled the cloth sack from Alecia's limp hands and rummaged around inside until he found the flint and tinderbox. The firewood he'd prepared yesterday was dry and soon a cheerful blaze dispersed the cold and shadows in the cave. The rustle of fabric made him turn to Alecia. The wariness in her gaze hurt.

"Good morning." His voice was harsher than he wanted.

Alecia flinched and drew her nightgown tighter. "Good morning."

He removed a pot from the sack and left the cave in search of water. The chore gave him more time to think, away from her presence. What was he to do? How had he become so entangled? Too soon, the pot was full of water and he headed back up the hill to the cave.

Alecia had tried to straighten her hair but the injuries to her face were what drew his eye. He placed the pot on the fire and knelt before her. "Are you well?"

"Tired," she said. "Where are we?"

"In a cave to the northeast of Brightcastle. It's not too late for you to return."

"No," she said. Just like that and without hesitation.

"I don't think you can stay with me."

"I made my choice," Alecia said. "I'll travel with you for as long as you'll allow it."

"It's not safe. The road will be long and hard."

"Last night you kept me safe. I'm not afraid."

Vard could see she lied. "You *are* frightened, and wise to be so."

"I think it's you who are afraid," she said, sparks snapping in her eyes.

"You're right. Frightened for your safety. Scared of what you'll give up if you stay with me. Even with Hetty's help…"

"Hetty? What do you mean?"

Vard frowned. Would it really help to explain what the witch had done? He so wanted Alecia but dared not hope she could be content with a life on the road. Honesty drove him to speak. "Your friend has enchanted this amulet." He held the stone up.

Alecia stared at the talisman, the rays of the early morning sun reflected in its crimson depths. "It has changed."

"The stone now aids my control more than it ever did. I can deny the bear. As long as I have it, I believe you're safe from any threat *I* pose."

"The wolf?"

"Yes, and the hawk."

Alecia's eyes glowed, her face coming alight as he had not seen it for days. "I've seen your hawk form. You're magnificent."

She leaned forward and the neck of her nightgown gaped. Vard closed his eyes, pushing the sight away, and rose to stand, gazing out at the forest below. Alecia joined him, placing her hand on his arm and turning him toward her.

"Don't you see what this means, Vard? I no longer need fear the bear."

"If that were the only obstacle...I'd be stupid to think you can accept what I am. Foolish to believe you could be happy with me."

"I can learn to accept what you are, Vard." Her eyes, looking up at him, held no artifice. Her soul was bared; all the fear, pain, hope and longing were evident in that lilac gaze. He licked his lips and her eyes followed the action, her tongue mimicking his unconsciously. He groaned.

"You don't know what you're saying." He raised his hand to stroke her face then stopped himself. He had to maintain control.

Alecia caught at his hand and placed it on her chest, on the bare skin above her breasts. She gasped as the action brought the familiar snap of chemistry. It was nearly Vard's undoing, but he pushed the flood of desire aside and forced himself to calm.

"Feel that," she said. "My heart beats because of you. Without you, I'd be dead now."

"That's nonsense," Vard snapped, his control slipping. He pulled his hand from her skin.

"It's pure fact," Alecia said. "You rescued me three times. You saved me from Finus and from myself. You've given me reason to live and hope. If you leave me, I'll truly have nothing. I love you, Vard. I know you feel something for me. Don't be afraid that you repulse me."

"It's not your feelings that scare me, Princess, but my own..." Vard's voice trailed off.

Alecia gaped like a fish out of water. She shook her head. "Even your contempt of me is preferable to a loveless marriage. I know what you saw last night, but I didn't welcome Finus's attention. I had lost hope. Somehow it didn't matter anymore."

Vard raised his hand and let it fall, his mind full of the scene he had witnessed back in the castle. Finus's hands on her, stroking places only a lover should. "When I entered that room and saw you with him, every particle screamed for me to turn and leave but I couldn't. It was torture."

Alecia clasped her hands over her heart, her breasts rising and falling with a force that stirred the hunger in his loins. Bright hope lit her lilac eyes.

"You do care for me," she breathed. "You must believe I hated every one of his kisses, every touch of his hands."

Anger rose up in Vard and a low wolf growl escaped before he could stop it. He placed his forefinger on Alecia's lips. "Don't speak of it."

She grasped his wrist and pulled his finger away. "I must make you understand. I had truly lost everything. It didn't matter what he did to my body because it was an empty shell. You rejected me and then I discovered your true essence. The shock was too much. Then to have Finus...Please tell me you forgive me."

Guilt slammed into Vard's gut; guilt at believing the worst, at putting her through this pain and at not telling her the truth of his purpose in Brightcastle. "There is nothing to forgive, Alecia." He must tell her everything but first she needed to listen to his heart.

He pulled her against his chest, his lips moving against her hair. "There's no one I admire more in this world than you. You're brave and beautiful, generous and caring…"

Alecia stared up at him. "You think I'm beautiful?"

His hand touched her throat. "Even in this grubby nightgown, with bruises over your face and neck and smelling like a wolf, you're beautiful to me."

"So these feelings that worry you are…?"

Vard groaned and pulled her closer to him. He tilted her head back, his thumb brushing the softness of her mouth. How could she still be so uncertain? Didn't she feel the fever of his heart just as he could feel hers? He lowered his lips to Alecia's and all coherent thought fled in that moment.

"I want you," he said, his mouth trailing down her throat, over the yellowing bruises. "I love you," he breathed, nibbling along the neck of her nightgown. "I need you," he said, nudging aside the bodice of her gown and kissing her nipple.

Alecia groaned and pushed her hips against his. "I've dreamed of hearing you say those words." His lips returned to crush hers, his tongue invading the soft warmth of her mouth. She arched her body against him and he moved his thigh between her legs, brushing her sex. Alecia sighed and wrapped herself around Vard's thigh, gripping his hips and thrusting against him.

He groaned. It would be so easy to allow this; to strip the clothes from her long limbs and give her what she demanded. He was ready to bring her into the fullness of womanhood, consummate the moment that had begun that day in the meadow with their first heady kiss. He pulled away. Alecia must know the whole truth.

"What's wrong?" she asked, a frown marring her brow and hurt in her eyes. She placed her palm on his chest and he closed his eyes against the longing that swept him. The moment passed and he looked fully into her soul, bared for him, exposed and vulnerable, trusting him as only a lover could.

"There is one more thing you must know," he said, holding her gaze, willing her to understand. "Before you sacrifice your virginity, you must have the truth about me."

Fear clouded her lilac gaze. "There's nothing you can tell me that will stop me from loving you, Vard. You were meant for me and I for you." She ran her fingers down his chest and a surge of pure lust choked him. *Oh Goddess, let her understand.* Let her forgive him.

"You must hear this." He broke contact and turned away, giving her the chance to react without him watching, allowing him to avoid the hurt he knew he'd see.

"I came to Brightcastle because I was hired to perform a task."

"I know that, Vard — "

"Please, Alecia, just listen. I don't know who hired me. The money was a handsome amount. I kept enough to fund my travel here and gave the rest to a priestess of the Mother. I was to travel to Brightcastle and take up a commission as captain in the prince's army and head of his personal guard."

"Vard —"

"I was to kill your father."

Silence greeted his words but the dull thump of her heart missed a beat and then raced away. Vard pushed on. "The prince is a poor leader, cruel to his people. I believed the assassination would serve my Defender principles. I deluded myself that I could, in good faith, murder Prince Zialni. I failed on both my first and second attempts. Doubt stayed my hand. I had become your protector and that duty was all-consuming. I couldn't hurt you by killing the one parent you had left; the man you loved above all others."

Vard faced the woman who had so fundamentally shifted his life focus.

Alecia gazed up at him, her eyes more serious than they had ever been. "You're wrong."

"I know I was wrong to accept that task. I've failed you in so many ways. Perhaps I'm unworthy of the title of Defender. I'm certainly not worthy of your love."

"I meant you're wrong about the man I love above all others." Alecia gazed up at him, close but not touching. "*You* are that man. I love everything about you; your strength, your integrity and, most of all, I love your very reason for living; this drive you have to protect the weak, the innocent. How could I not love you, Vard? I feel the same; I always have. We'll protect them together."

Vard frowned. "You forgive me?"

"You didn't know what you agreed to, and your goodness, your caring, stopped you from acting. There's nothing to forgive. Now, make love to me." She pulled loose the ribbon at the neck of her nightgown and the garment dropped from her body. The pantaloons joined the gown and Alecia stood in the gentle light of the morning sun: full breasts, long legs, slim waist and soft, soft skin.

It was all his for the taking, but he didn't go to her. He just looked, allowing days – no, weeks – of need to push him to the peak of longing. Vard delayed the moment when they would be one, almost afraid to cross that line, wondering what he'd find beyond it.

But Alecia stepped close and wrapped her arms around his neck, resting her glorious curves against his taut length. The trust and love in her eyes stole his breath, and his body responded, his arms curling about her waist. He wrapped one hand in the length of her golden hair and gently pulled, tilting her head so the soft expanse of her neck was exposed. A pulse beat there, strong and fast and charged with excitement.

Vard gasped at the rush of desire that hit him, wrapped around his chest, smashed at his loins. He brought his mouth to ravish the bruised skin where her life force beat. Alecia moaned and pushed her hips against him, but his mouth continued down to her chest, over her breasts to her nipples. The magnificent flesh was hard with need and grew ever harder as his tongue flicked, his lips sucked.

His fingers trailed to her waist then drifted lower and she wrapped one leg around him, giving him ready access to her sex. His fingers entered her and she gasped, shuddering against him. He found the core of her desire, the hard spot that pulsed with a life of its own, and he ran his finger over it, delighting in her shuddering sighs until she let out one long moan and her body melted into him. Vard held her, supported her supple flesh as she breathed heavily in the aftermath of her climax.

Finally, Alecia looked up at him. He raised one eyebrow and she blushed.

"That was...that was... I never imagined how it could feel." She beamed up at him and Vard's heart swelled with love for his princess.

A sudden frown marred the soft skin of her brow. "I need to be one with you."

Vard grasped her shoulders as she pushed forward against him again. He held her apart. "You're sure this is what you want, Alecia? Once you take this step, all will change. You'll be a woman, and I don't think I'll be able to walk away."

Alecia's smile lit her face, her hungry lilac eyes firing the slow burn in his loins. "I'm your destiny."

All the barriers Vard had carefully constructed came crashing down, and he crushed her to his chest. Words clogged his throat, so he showed her the depth of his love instead. His lips met hers in one long, tender, soul-affirming kiss that deepened until Alecia moaned, allowing his tongue to explore the deepest reaches of her mouth. Her fingers wove through his hair, tugging gently, stirring his desire until he couldn't wait any longer.

Vard pulled his mouth from Alecia's long enough to spread her discarded nightgown at the front of the cave. He lifted her in his arms and she laughed as he gently laid her on the garment. He bent to kiss her again but her frantic hands tugged at his clothes. Vard stood, slowly peeling off his tunic and then his breeches and hose, until he stood naked before her.

Alecia's eyes widened at his nudity, her heartbeat exploding into a gallop in time with his own.

"Love me," she whispered.

He knelt and kissed her neck, her shoulders and her breasts until she strained against him, begging for release. Then his hand slid beneath her buttocks and he entered her, slowly, gently, until all of him was consumed in her warmth. Alecia tensed at the pressure but then moved against him, meeting him thrust for thrust until she groaned and stiffened around him, sparking his release, his seed exploding inside her.

Afterwards as they lay entwined, Vard marvelled at the depth of his feelings. Alecia was part of him, and right at that moment he wanted to stay joined with her for eternity. "I love you," he said.

"And I you," she said. "I'd stay like this forever but I fear the world will eventually intrude."

"And what then?"

"I won't go back." Alecia smoothed his forehead with her fingers.

"You can't abandon your people."

"We'll help them together and find a Defender to teach you."

Vard gazed down at his princess, her face lit with the smile that made her irresistible. "In this moment, I really believe we can achieve all that."

"We can, Vard. You'll see."

Vard smiled. With this woman by his side, anything was possible.

Epilogue

SQUIRE Ramón Zorba stalked back and forth across the entrance to Brightcastle Keep. If he had been a cat, his tail would have been lashing. As it was, the only lashing had come from his employer, Prince Zialni. The royal blamed him, Ramón, for the kidnapping of his daughter, Alecia. By some means, Zialni discerned that Ramón was not altogether innocent of the charge of aiding Anton when he fled the castle last night with the princess.

He ground his teeth so hard he half expected them to crack under the strain. If only he had stopped Anton when given the chance, but Alecia had been persuasive and he had been caught, literally, with his pants down. Still, Anton was a blade master and Ramón, though skilled, was no match for the man. Perhaps he had taken the only sensible path last eve, but that would be scant comfort in the long days ahead.

It didn't matter that he raised the alarm as soon as he could throw on his clothes; had summoned the guards and dogs and sent the force to precisely where the blasted fugitive would exit the castle. They had nearly caught them but, moments from success, the couple vanished like smoke on the wind. They were there one moment and gone the next. The horses panicked, and the dogs whimpered and shied away from the patch of forest Anton escaped into with Alecia. Had he used witchcraft? Or did he have another means of escape? Ramón had long thought there was something alien about Anton.

Several hours of beating around in the dark forest northeast of the castle produced nothing but frustration. When he and commander

Vorasava reported their lack of progress to the prince, he was furious. Add to that the princess's betrothed on death's door and it had been a dark twenty-four hours for Brightcastle.

Ramon didn't know how Alecia came to be in the keep when he had been told the prince sent her away for her safety. His head ached with keeping straight what he knew and the secrets he must never tell. He had seen the princess when she returned from the cells, the night he begged her to come away with him, pleaded with her to give their relationship a chance. She had been battered and bruised, almost beyond recognition. The damage would take weeks to heal.

Prince Zialni couldn't afford to allow anyone to see his daughter like that. Once the tongues of the gossips wagged, it wouldn't be long before someone guessed the princess was responsible for the mercenary murders.

But why had she acted as she did? He may never discover the truth and certainly couldn't ask his employer. Alecia possessed a core of honor and goodness, he knew that much. If she attacked the sell swords, they must have earned it, must have done something deserving of their end. But what?

He couldn't believe Alecia capable of such action. Oh, she was skilled in weapons and an athletic young woman, but that was a long stretch from the audacity and bravery she had shown by challenging three armed men.

Prince Zialni could not allow the populace to know his daughter had acted in such a way or he would never find a husband for her. His thoughts turned to Lord Finus, who hovered between life and death, according to the prince. It had been less than a week since Alecia's betrothal and now those plans lay a smoking wreck. No wonder Prince Zialni was furious.

So furious he was now leading the search party for his daughter, while Ramón had been left in charge of the Keep, with a skeleton guard to keep the peace. Twenty-four years of age and he was being treated as a disobedient child. It was Vard Anton's fault, not Alecia's. She merely acted to secure her freedom, taking any help that presented itself. If he had known how dire her mental anguish was, he'd have spirited her away himself. He didn't know what his next steps would've been, but anything was better than the current situation.

Yes, if he ever had another chance, he'd make it up to Alecia and ensure she enjoyed the future she longed for, with a man worthy of her. And that man was Ramón Zorba.

THE END

GLOSSARY

Places

Kingdom of Thorius (Thor- ee- us) -the kingdom of men which encompasses the King's seat of Wildecoast and the Prince's seat of Brightcastle, along with other smaller towns

Wildecoast (Will – dee – coast) -the capital city perched on the top of a cliff overlooking the sea on the east coast of Thorius; climate is mild but windy

Brightcastle - large inland town surrounded by forests and farms, three to four days ride west of Wildecoast

Amitania (Am – it – ay – nia) or *Elvandang* (Elle – van – dang) in elvish - the deserted city north of the Usetar Mountain Range in northern Thorius; once a thriving city; disputed ownership between elves and man

Usetar Range (You – set – ar) -the mountain range running across the northern parts of Thorius

People

Lenweri (Len – weir – ee) -the elven people who are tall and elegant with black skin and pointed ears and mainly dark hair; live in mountainous forests north and west of Thorius, in places encroaching onto Kingdom lands; also known as dark elves

Sis Lenweri - the faction of dark elves that wishes to take the kingdom of Thorius back from men

Defender - a race of shapeshifters who are created to defend those in danger; they sense those in need of their help; a Defender can shift into animal form and the ability is inherited through family lines

Characters

Princess Alecia Zialni (Al – ee – sha Zee – al – nee)) - the King's niece and daughter of Prince Jiseve Zialni who rules the principality of Brightcastle and is next in line to the throne. Alecia's story begins in Princess Avenger and continues in Princess in Exile.

Vard Anton - a shapeshifting Defender; army captain of Brightcastle in Princess Avenger; holder of many secrets; his story continues in Princess in Exile

Prince Jiseve Zialni (Jiss – eve Zee – al – nee) - next in line to the throne of Thorius, younger brother of the King, a widower; father of Alecia Zialni

Ramón Zorba (Rah – mon Zor – bah) - Lord of Wildecoast and squire to Prince Jiseve Zialni; his family have an estate south of Wildecoast

Hetty – mysterious ancient woman with magical powers; once Alecia's governess and nanny; declared a witch by Prince Jiseve and sentenced to death but rescued by Alecia

King Beniel Zialni (Ben – ee – elle Zee – al – nee) - King of Thorius; lives in Wildecoast; older brother of Jiseve Zialni and uncle of Alecia Zialni; married to Adriana

Queen Adriana - wife of the King; lives in Wildecoast; Alecia's aunt

Jacques Vorasava - Lieutenant in the Brightcastle army

Lord Giornan Finus (Jor – nan Fie – nus) – recently come to Brightcastle from a neighboring kingdom; Jiseve Zialni's advisor

Jorge Andra (George Andra) – previous squire to Prince Jiseve and close friend to Alecia; killed by mercenaries who were trying to collect money from his parents

Piotr Zialni (Peter Zialni) – son of Beniel and Jiseve Zialni's younger brother; next in line to the throne of Thorius (his father is dead) unless the King, Prince or Alecia have a son.

Izebel (Is – zee – belle) – a previous warrior Queen of Thorius from centuries ago, when females could rule; Alecia's idol.

ABOUT THE AUTHOR

Bernadette Rowley is a lover of epic fantasy who is a veterinarian by day and an author by night. She is currently published in the genre of high fantasy romance with eight books, all set in her fantasy world of Thorius.

When she was a young teenager, an aunt gave her a copy of The Sword of Shannara by Terry Brooks and Bernadette has lived in various fantasy worlds ever since. It's no surprise that her chosen genre when writing romance is fantasy.

"I can see these settings so vibrantly in my mind and hope my readers can too."

But Bernadette has no desire to spoon-feed her readers by laboriously describing her fantasy settings. She would rather the reader use their own imagination.

Along with sword and sorcery, dashing heroes and stunning heroines, this author includes strong healing themes in many of her books- an element central to her everyday job.

"When I started writing the Queenmakers Saga, I never imagined my day job would force its way into my stories as it has."

And of course, there are animals, especially Bernadette's beloved horses.

Bernadette lives in Brisbane, Australia, with the four heroes in her life- her husband Michael and three grown sons.

Connect with the Author

Website: www.bernadetterowley.com
Facebook: www.facebook.com/bernadetterowleyfantasy
Twitter: www.twitter.com/bt_rowley

Made in the USA
Middletown, DE
12 October 2020

21780184R00115